TAMMY PLUNKETT

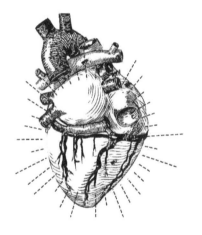

CLINICAL TRIAL

Big Sky Authors Ltd.
Airdrie AB, Canada
info@bigskyauthorservices.com

Tammy Plunkett, author
Tami Hutchinson, cover art
Zoey Duncan, editor

ISBN 978-1-7773152-1-4   Paperback
ISBN 978-1-7773152-0-7   eBook

First Edition

To Rod, with all my love.

Chapter 1

"I can't suture ground beef."

Dr. Georgia Laurence stared at the lump of immobile heart tissue inside the cavernous hole in Ms. Jenkins' chest. Her own heartbeat roared in her ears. A tiny swirl of smoke rose from the end of the cauterizing wand in her resident's hand, stinging her nostrils with the scent of burning flesh.

"There's nothing left to do." She dropped her scalpel into a metal basin with a clang. "I have to close this woman up and tell her I can't do a damn thing."

Georgia didn't look at the nurses, residents, and anesthetist team, but she could feel their anticipation and knew what they were waiting for. Her eruptions arrived like clockwork after a bad day in the OR. She tried her damnedest not to give in to them, but those cathartic words simmered below the surface. No way was she going to let her chief resident win this bet. At last, she improvised.

"Oh, F.O.R.K. Fork! Fork it all!"

And operating room two at Albany's Our Lady of Grace Hospital came back to life as if a pause button had been released.

"I didn't think you had it in you, Dr. L." Dr. Joe Carter's blue eyes crinkled above his mask.

"Yeah, well, our bet is off for the rest of the day now." She rolled her eyes at Joe, her chief resident, and returned to the more important issue at hand—the patient on her table. Sandra Jenkins needed the valve on the left side of her heart replaced. It had prolapsed to the point where her blood back flowed and caused her heart to fail. The heart tissue was so damaged there was nothing for Georgia to stitch a new valve into.

Her feet throbbed from standing for the last five hours between morning rounds and trying to do something to give Ms. Jenkins her life back. Georgia clasped her gloved hands in front of her. "I don't even have anything here to attach a temporary pump, like an LVAD. How the hell is this woman still circulating her blood?"

"Right now, she's not," said the oh-so-ready-to-retire perfusionist with a snicker, sitting at the six-by-eight-foot machine that was doing the work of Ms. Jenkins' heart and lungs during the surgery.

"Ha-ha. You're a bag o' laughs this morning, aren't you? You'd better keep your fingers crossed that she comes off the heart-lung machine at all." Georgia turned to the circulating nurse. "Get the surgical ICU team leader on the phone. Tell her she's getting one hell of a sick lady and I want her best nurse."

The operating room was kept cool and dry on purpose—to keep down the growth of mold and bacteria—but standing under those hot lights always made Georgia feel like an order of nuggets and fries waiting for pick-up. The overhead lamps beamed down on the rib-spreader and surrounding sterile sheets. Georgia stared at the light patterns on the metal bars while she tried to weigh all the options before her. The LVAD—left ventricular assist device—would have hooked up to the heart and done the heart's work for it, but in this case, Ms. Jenkins' heart muscle acted more like an over-stretched elastic on a pair of Fruit of the Looms. It wouldn't contract.

Georgia's gaze drifted to her patient's face. That inoperable organ belonged to a stoic, upstanding woman who, even under anesthesia, managed to look determined, as if failure wasn't an option. When Georgia met Ms. Jenkins in her office for the pre-operative check-up, she'd stood tall, wearing a pretty yellow blouse and pencil skirt, her hair in neat braids that covered her head, holding the hand of a girl dressed in a private school uniform. Ms. Jenkins was a 42-year-old, single mom, and a hard-working accountant who spent most of her days at a desk, which explained why she ignored her symptoms and allowed her heart to get so bad. She clearly cared very deeply for her daughter and wanted to provide for her. She barely winced when Georgia pried her shoes from her swollen ankles to look for a pulse. Georgia wanted to know the secret of how this woman had made it this far, and with a polite smile on her face all the while.

Pulling her thoughts back to the present, Georgia still had no miracle cures. The OR staff were getting antsy for a plan.

"I've never seen anything this bad before, Dr. Laurence," Brian, a bright-eyed first-year resident offered. "It's a miracle this woman is alive at all. She's hanging on by a thread."

Joe cut in before Georgia had a chance. "This isn't show and tell. Stop gawking and come up with some bright ideas. You're the one all up on his theory lessons." Take no prisoners. Like most surgeons—and pilots and quarterbacks—he was gifted with both ability and a chiseled jaw. She appreciated that he didn't let his looks and white, male privilege disrupt his important work. Not only was Joe smart, he was devoted and worked harder than most of the residents who had passed through the OR doors, which was saying a lot because heart surgery was a passion, not a make-ends-meet kind of job.

"All I can think of is a heart transplant," Brian said as he stepped away from the table.

"And that's all I can think of too," Georgia said. "Sophie, call the transplant coordinator and tell her to meet us in SICU."

The anesthetist perked up and cleared his throat. "We're closing her up, then?"

Everyone knew he had a standing date with a set of golf clubs.

Georgia bit her lip behind her surgical mask and pulled on the purse-string suture as she removed the cannula from the pulmonary vein. "Let's see how Ms. Jenkins likes pumping her oxygenated blood around." She repeated the suture on the aortic root, unclamped the aorta, and held her breath. The temporary pacemaker started the heart. The ventilator inflated the lungs.

"Looking good. I see a nice wave of pink flushing this sad, overworked heart. See any leaks, Joe?"

"All's good from this side."

"Okay, let's see if she can hold her own rhythm." Georgia turned off the pacemaker so Ms. Jenkins' heart could resume its duty. It did. Georgia's shoulders dropped with relief.

"Great. Let's close her up."

Georgia turned to the scrub nurse. "Can I get a dab on the forehead? And a 1.0 silk? Thanks."

"Georgia, we've got lots of premature ventricular contractions over here," announced the anesthetist.

Damn it. If one of those irregular heartbeats fell on the wrong phase of her intrinsic rhythm, they were screwed. Ventricular fibrillation would be a death sentence on an already struggling heart. "What were her last electrolytes?" Georgia demanded.

"They were good," said the circulating nurse.

Georgia swiveled from the heart fighting to contract in front of her to the readings on the heart monitor. A single bead of sweat trickled down her back.

"Shit, she's in V-fib. Give me biphasic shocks starting at two kilojoules."

The nurse wheeled over the defibrillator machine and cranked the dial. Everyone stepped back from the table as the machine juiced up. "Clear!" Georgia yelled as she placed the long-handled paddles on either ventricle and pushed the buttons with her thumbs.

The OR staff's gazes were riveted to the monitor's sharp-pointed, wide waveforms.

"Christ, nothing. Five kilojoules. Come on, Ms. J." There was no way Georgia was going to call a time of death today. But five kilojoules did nothing either. "Crank it up to seven kilojoules." Again, nothing.

In her periphery, Georgia could see the anesthetist administering the typical medications given in a cardiac arrest. The nurse off in the corner charted the procedures. Georgia held Ms. Jenkins' heart in her gloved hand and massaged it to allow the medications to pump through it. There was no time left to waste.

"Give me the fucking paddles and put it up to twenty," she ordered.

"You didn't do ten," Joe said.

"I know, just crank it up, and—clear." Georgia momentarily held her breath every time she pushed the buttons. "Let's go, you useless piece of shit heart. Beat for Christ's sake. Clear!" A normal heart rhythm marched across the screen and a wave of sighs filled the room. Georgia's own racing heart rushed blood to her arms and hands, making them tingle.

"Now, can someone please light a fire under the transplant team's ass?" Joe barked. "This won't last very long."

* * *

Bed three's cubicle in the surgical intensive care unit overflowed with machines and nurses as everyone jostled to get Ms. Jenkins stabilized, which finally happened late in the afternoon. The nurse's station also buzzed with a throng of blood-typing specialists and the transplant team all looking for what they needed for the perfect match.

An exhausted Georgia had just typed her last charting note for the day at the nursing station when she saw Carol Hawking, the transplant coordinator, walking toward her looking grim. Georgia could feel her forehead crease.

"Things aren't looking hopeful," Carol said straight out, hands shoved into her lab coat pockets. "Despite Ms. Jenkins' condition, we still have three people on LVAD who take priority."

Georgia slammed the lid on her laptop. "That is such bullshit! The only reason she's not on LVAD herself is that she's beyond critical. That puts her at the top of the damned list, and you know it."

"Sorry, it's nationwide protocol. My hands are tied. Besides, you know how rare an AB-positive blood type is and it seems your patient has some very rare antibodies too. The tests aren't all back, but it's not looking promising at all."

Georgia wanted to get mad at someone, anyone, to relieve the frustration about to explode, but she had worked with Carol in the past and she knew she meant well. That didn't mean she had to like the news though.

"That's it? You're giving up before we've even started to look?"

"No, Dr. Laurence. Not at all. I just want to be honest with you about the situation and our odds. I'll get back to you in the morning with the final analysis."

"Yeah, thanks." Georgia threaded a hand through her hair as she watched Carol leave the nurses' station. Part of her wanted to scream in frustration; another part wanted to crawl under the covers and hide for the night. It seemed the harder she fought for Ms. Jenkins, the more obstacles got thrown into her path. She wasn't normally a huge believer in fate, but she was finding it tougher by the minute to ignore the writing on the wall. She blinked back tears and sat taller, remembering all the staff around.

* * *

Georgia tossed her house keys on the pile of unopened boxes of books that served as an entry table and kicked off her shoes. She really needed to make a trip to Pottery Barn and get some more furniture for this place.

Hands on hips, she glared at the dog stretched out on the couch in the living room. "Still not talking to me, Gus? You know, most dogs rush to the front door to greet their owners."

Her faithful companion twitched his floppy ear at the sound of his name but otherwise didn't bother to move. The bloodhound was no fool, he knew how to get affection from her, just play hard to get. She walked over to him and scratched behind his right ear, and as a reward, Gus made eye contact for a millisecond before rolling over.

Georgia collapsed onto the bit of couch space beside him and lifted his head onto her lap. She buried her face in his neck, letting out all the tears of frustration that had accumulated behind her professional bravado. As the weight of the day poured out of her, Gus rearranged himself to lay his head on her chest, his sad expression mirroring her mood. Despite her tears, Georgia felt the corners of her mouth twitch. It was hard to stay sad in the face of such comic mournfulness. She ruffled his ears and stretched her arm across him to retrieve the remote control wedged into the cushions at the far end of the couch. It didn't even occur to her, however, to suggest he move out of the way.

The couch belonged to Gus as much as to Georgia for two reasons: first, because no one else ever came around and second, because Gus said it did. But Georgia didn't mind, because on it, and with him, was where she could let go of the stress of her job. She inherited Gus from her best friend Emma, who was a child psychologist. He was trained as a therapy dog and did wonders for Emma—and her anxious clients—until Emma needed a little more than puppy love to get through some tough shit. There was little Georgia could do to fix Emma's life at the time and inheriting what Georgia considered just an overfed oaf hadn't felt much like helping. But having a good home for Gus made Emma happy and within a week of living together, Gus owned both Georgia's couch and her heart.

She got up and turned on the television to the weather network. It was pretty much the only channel she ever watched because she hated the news and didn't have time to get hooked on a series and miss half the episodes. This way she could see what the weather had looked like while she was holed up in the hospital—sometimes for eighteen hours a day—or so she could dress appropriately for her runs. The weather rarely kept her from a good jog, and the late start to summer this year made running a bit more pleasant than the hot and humid crap she was sure would come by July or August.

She walked over and opened her refrigerator to find a barren interior. Either the dog walker had eaten all her food, or the housekeeper had completely ignored her grocery list.

"Pizza or Chinese, Gus?"

Silence.

"Pizza it is."

She opened the food delivery app on her phone and flipped through pizza options. The last time she had pizza was at her friend Jody's house celebrating her daughter's third birthday. All everyone talked about was the challenges of getting into the right pre-school. Georgia had felt so out of her element. At the age of thirty-three, convention dictated she should be married with babies spitting up all over her and pulling on Gus's ears, but she'd given that up in pursuit of her goal to highlight and fix heart disease in women. And what did she have to show for it? Eating alone with a hand-me-down dog.

Georgia shook off the newest layer of melancholy, reminding herself that this was exactly what she wanted. She'd learned early on how much heart disease was overlooked in women and how fragile and fleeting family could be. Her life already overflowed with responsibilities and people who depended on her. The last thing she needed was a family depending on her too. A child with a mother too preoccupied to raise her properly? No, thank you. Georgia wasn't lonely. It was the dog that was lonely. Georgia was damned proud of the sacrifices she'd made in her years of study and practice.

In the end, though, it appeared that all her years of studying and self-sacrifice still weren't enough to help her patient. Right now, what Ms. Jenkins really needed was someone crazy enough to hop on a motorcycle without a helmet and get into a horrible accident, because at this point, no matter how much Georgia had learned or how much she'd perfected her skills, she couldn't help Ms. Jenkins until someone else died.

Georgia mindlessly scrolled through social media on her phone. She was usually fairly good at leaving work at work, but she just couldn't get Ms. Jenkins off her mind. Maybe because she admired the woman so much. A single mother who'd fought her whole life to rise above the projects she came from. A woman who'd achieved a great feat by establishing herself in a well-paid career so her daughter Shawna could go to the best private schools and have all the opportunities Ms. Jenkins herself never got. And now she was slipping away with no family to care for Shawna, other than Ms. Jenkins' troubled sister. It would mean Shawna was bound for the foster system if her mother passed.

No way on Earth would Shawna end up in the foster care system if Georgia had anything to do with it. She'd only met the girl for a few minutes, but Georgia could see how caring and inquisitive she was. Besides, Georgia knew all too well that a mother could never be replaced.

Her stomach rumbled, reminding her of why she stood in her kitchen with her phone in her hand. She managed to start clicking on her pizza selections in the app before the phone started to ring. Joe Carter's name popped onto the display.

She'd worked side by side with her chief resident for three years and knew there wasn't much Joe couldn't handle, so having him call on her night off didn't bode well. She gave Gus a sad glance and swiped to answer.

"Hey, Joe. What's up?"

"Hey, Dr. L. What's for dinner?"

"I haven't ordered yet. Tell me you're not really calling me about my dinner choices."

"Yes and no," he said. "I've been thinking about something all afternoon and holding out on you, but I think it's time. I have something special to share with you. It's a little, how can I put it, unconventional? How about picking up some Chinese and meeting me in your office?"

"What the hell are you talking about, Joe? I just left." She threw a hand in the air dramatically for Gus' sake. This was completely out of character for Joe. He knew how important it was for her to reset after a day like today.

"Listen, I don't want to get into it over the phone, but it has to do with Ms. Jenkins. Trust me."

Georgia relented.

"Moo goo gai pan?" she asked.

14

"You know me too well."

She hung up and walked over to pet Gus. "If Joe and I start finishing each other's sentences, chew off my arm. Maybe I do need to start dating because I am way too available to go back to work."

Gus bounced off the couch with his whole hind end wagging and sat in front of her with the most alert expression she'd seen on the dog in a year. Was that a twinkle in the old hound's eye?

"Look, I'm not going manhunting tonight, so you can go back to being an oaf." Gus's jowls dropped. He grunted and returned to his couch. "I'm not going to marry the first guy to come along just to make you happy. How pathetic do you think I am?"

* * *

Georgia dropped the bag of takeout onto her desk and pulled out a couple of steaming cardboard containers. "This better be good," she said. "And I'm totally adding this to the money you owe me for today's bet."

She flicked on the only the two lamps in the room, leaving the overhead lights off and the window blinds open. Working as many night shifts as Joe did, his body needed the lighting cues to keep his melatonin levels in check.

Joe sat in the seat across from Georgia's desk, making room for his dinner between piles of journals and file folders. "Okay, here's the deal," he said. "You can't replace Ms. Jenkins' mitral valve again because you have nothing but Jell-O for heart tissue to sew it into."

"Can we get to the part I don't know?" She said as she handed him a box and chopsticks.

"What if you could give her new heart tissue?" he asked, tapping his temple with the chopsticks.

"The only way to do that is with a heart transplant, and

that would come with a healthy mitral valve of its own. Besides, she's already on the transplant list. You're not giving me anything new here." She leaned back and rubbed her tired eyes.

"All right. How's this for new?" He leaned across the desk. "What if she grew her own new heart tissue?"

Georgia frowned. "You mean with stem cells? That research is at least another five years away from being used in humans. She'll be lucky if she gets five days." Not only had he dragged her back to work for this crap, he'd stolen her almond cookie while she spoke.

"Maybe not," he said, a mischievous grin lighting up his face. "Know where they're doing the animal trials? Right here in Our Lady of Grace. My old roommate from Larner College is the senior lab assistant. We had lunch together today, and he told me all about the clinical trial. They're curing chronic heart failure and repairing damaged heart tissue after heart attacks."

"In pigs," Georgia pointed out.

"You know how close a pig's heart is to a human's." Joe shrugged off her objection. "We use their valves in our patients all the time. Besides, they're also getting human heart tissue to grow in petri dishes."

Georgia put down her food and leaned in, curiosity taking over. Stem cells were coming a long way to develop therapies to repair damaged organ tissue. "How far off does your friend think human trials are?"

"Any time now. They're looking for low-risk candidates for the human trials," he mumbled around a bite of her stolen almond cookie.

"Yeah, well, 'low-risk' doesn't fit Ms. Jenkins by any stretch of the imagination." She picked up the container of noodles and shoveled one last bite into her mouth. She leaned back in the chair and swung her feet onto her desk.

"No," Joe agreed, "but I was thinking with your pretty brown eyes and the pull your name has, you might be able to get around those minor details. Ken told me there have been some issues with funding not coming in regularly, which might motivate the research team to move a little faster. Publishing their study will definitely help with cashflow."

"You're suggesting I use my position and feminine wiles to push a researcher into taking on a risky case?"

Joe grinned, unabashed. "Yup."

A huge sigh escaped her. She had nothing else to offer Ms. Jenkins besides the transplant list. Even if Joe's suggestion really could work, she couldn't break her personal code of ethics—she'd never use sex to get ahead. Women had to fight hard enough to be taken seriously in surgery without giving anybody a reason to say they didn't deserve their spot.

"I'm not going to sleep my way to saving lives."

"I never said to sleep with the guy," Joe said.

She rubbed her face with both hands and sighed again. Then again, was a life not worth more than her pride? She was sick and tired of letting death claim beautiful young women with their whole lives ahead of them, tired of families left behind with gaping holes in their souls. Surely, she could bat her pretty brown eyes at some old lab dweller in exchange for a chance to see Ms. Jenkins live and raise her daughter. Hell, she might even put on a push-up bra first.

She eyed her chief resident across the desk. "Whose ass am I going to have to kiss to get this to happen?"

"The very influential ass of Dr. Matt Mancini."

"Oh, shit."

Chapter 2

Georgia went straight to the elevators that led to the research wing. She hadn't dealt directly with a Mancini in about a million years, and she'd have been grateful if it had been a million more. So why had her heart skipped a beat as soon as she heard Matt's name? And why was it doing the same thing now, steps from his office? She scowled. Traitorous thing.

She saw him before she knocked. He was shutting down his computer while shrugging off his lab coat. The office was rich mahogany and hunter green, exactly as she would expect the heir of a medical empire's office to be. Decorated with the whims of someone who'd clearly never had to pick out furnishings at a thrift store and reminding her of how the Mancini family had always made her feel.

She'd met Matt's father first, the renowned Dr. John Mancini, who'd patented a revolutionary method of doing a hip replacement and made millions. Dr. John was her supervisor during her ortho rotation in med school, brilliant and absolutely full of himself. Then she met Phil, Matt's brother and Georgia's first love. Unfortunately, their whirlwind, short-lived love affair had ended with as much hate as the lust that started it. Phil, who had followed in their father's footsteps by going into orthopedic surgery, and John graced the halls of Our Lady of Grace about once a month on consults, but she usually managed to avoid them both by living in the OR and surgical intensive care.

She had run into Matt only a couple of times when she was dating Phil. Matt was way better looking than his younger brother, but he wasn't the partying type, so he and Phil ran in different circles. Matt was older, wiser, and only had deep and meaningful conversations with Georgia when they did speak, which wasn't often. She had always been curious about the serious older brother recalling his fascination with microbiology. She had been way too infatuated by Phil at the time to realize she had more in common with Matt while pretending to be a party girl for Phil's sake.

She knocked and he stopped mid-motion. He turned and flashed a brilliant smile, and for a second, she was transported to eight years earlier when his brother's smile could give her goosebumps across the room. Matt's smile was different—none of the sneer she only came to recognize later in that relationship with Phil.

"Dr. Mancini," was all she got out of her dry mouth. No one, not even Georgia herself, could ever imagine her speechless. She internally cursed at herself as she wiped the sweat off her hands.

He raised an eyebrow. "What has you wandering around the research wing tonight, Dr. Laurence?"

"Georgia, please."

"It's been a long time." He extended his hand and when his strong, warm palm touched hers, she feared her whole body would melt. "Last time I saw you was when you and Phil graduated. I've been meaning to come by and say hello since I took the job here, but I rarely leave the research wing. I can't believe it's been almost two years since I took the position here. You here for news about Phil?" His shirt had obviously been tailored for him. It hugged his chest and skimmed his shoulders and caressed his abs, just as she would like to—no. She was here for business. For Ms. Jenkins.

"No. I was looking for you. But you seem to be heading out." Phil who? How crazy blind had she been to Matt? Why on Earth did she waste her time dating Phil?

"I've been here all day," he said. "I need some air."

"Mind if I walk you out? I have some questions about your research," she said, doing her best not to hyperventilate. What was wrong with her?

"Sure."

Georgia started to doubt her ability to convince Matt to save Ms. Jenkins' life. It was a struggle to string together a coherent sentence, so how was she going to turn on the charm and convince a man who had it all—money, looks, success, talent, and one hell of a gorgeous ass—to listen to her?

Outside, warm late spring air filled Georgia's lungs, replacing the stale hospital air.

"So, what do you want to know?" Matt asked as they walked along the path toward the park.

"I'm embarrassed to say that I don't know much about the research we have going on here. I was wondering if you'd enlighten me on your clinical trial."

"The one where I collected heart cell samples from your patients? We finished that six months ago. The article will be published next month."

"You collected samples from my patients?" She stopped under a streetlamp and turned to him.

"Not personally, well, except once—when my research nurse, Judy, was on vacation."

She remembered Judy now, and she recalled signing off on the paperwork for the samples. She peered into his eyes, the only part of him she'd be able to identify if he had come into her OR masked and gowned. No sparks of recollection buzzed in her brain, but flutters ran amok in her peritoneum.

"What are you working on now?" She continued their walk toward the lake.

"Mildred." He grinned.

"Pardon?"

"I'm growing myocardial stem cells from skin tissue, and we implanted a batch into our last animal's cardiac tissue today hoping the cells reproduce and repair her heart. Mildred is a pig. We've teamed with a group in California. They've got all the financial backing, but we've got a governor who's pushing for research advances."

They reached Washington Park and sat on a bench overlooking the water. The streetlights twinkled on the lake and the evening silence was cut with the occasional swish of rollerblades and the steady slap of running shoes on the path behind them.

Georgia caught herself admiring his features. The past few years had treated him very well. The intelligence in his dark blue eyes surrounded by the tiniest of laugh lines and the slightest graying of his jet-black hair betrayed a maturity that the rest of his fit body denied. She gave herself a mental head shake. Where's the ruthless heart surgeon now? She wasn't used to this amount of physical distraction. Enough eye candy, back to business.

"How far along are you in the process?"

"Mildred is our last animal subject. Now we wait for the higher-ups to be satisfied. They give us the go-ahead for human testing or they ask for more animal trials. I wouldn't mind doing two or three more pigs myself. If that's the case, I'd say about six months to a year if anyone gets squeamish, and then we'll be onto humans."

Georgia twisted her hands in her lap, she should have known that Matt would be risk-averse with his trial.

"We'll probably do about twenty-five to thirty human subjects before the trial is over, and if all works out, you'll be working with stem cells on your patients to repair heart muscle in less than ten years." He crossed his ankle onto his knee and leaned back.

She hoped her face didn't fall when she felt her shoulders drop. Acting wasn't her strong suit. "That long? And are your higher-ups making a conscious choice of including women in your human trials?"

"Ah, yes, that's your area of expertise, I remember now. I'm happy to see your passion for women's cardiac health hasn't waned. I will be sure to put in a word with the oversight team."

"Thanks. Here I was hoping to get you started on a female human candidate tonight." She flashed a half-hearted smile.

He grinned, turned away, and stared at the lake in front of them, and she wondered if what she said came off as the truth or as a joke. She wasn't sure how she meant it herself.

"And if the higher-ups are satisfied, when do you expect to start human trials?" she asked.

"The protocol is ready. We just need to find the right candidates. I guess you'll get to know my research nurse very well in the next little while," he said.

"What constitutes the right candidate?" She knew the answer to her question before she posed it but hoped beyond hope she was wrong.

"Low-risk, and very healthy in all other regards. We don't want to skew our good results with cases that could die during the research."

Georgia turned her head to roll her eyes at a nearby bush. Practicing medicine on healthy people for the sake of a good-looking clinical trial. Makes total sense. Not. How could a good doctor turn his back on a dying patient? Could Matt refuse a candidate if he saw her desperation?

Georgia sure as hell couldn't buy Matt off. Maybe sleeping with him really would help? After all, those strong hands sure would look good on—no, Georgia. That's not how you practice medicine. Maybe she could convince him of extenuating circumstances for Ms. Jenkins?

"I was wondering if you'd join me on rounds tomorrow morning. I have a patient I'd like your expertise on." She stood, bringing a symbolic end to their little talk and an escape route from the direction of her racy train of thought.

"My expertise?"

"Ms. Jenkins is a terminal heart patient. I can explain more in the morning. Bed three, in surgical intensive care. Seven o'clock."

"Um, okay." He stood to meet her gaze.

"Nice talking with you, Matt." She offered an officious handshake. Her jaw ached from clenching it to keep professionalism at the forefront.

He turned back toward the hospital parking lot, probably headed for his Jaguar or BMW. She headed for her condo two blocks away. They were totally different species— he, a cure-chaser hiding behind an electron microscope, and she, a surgeon on the cutting edge. He came from a long line of money and doctors—the Kennedys of medicine. She was still paying off her student loans eight years after residency.

Matt's brother and father had always made her feel like Cinderella who should be grateful to be invited to their ball. And now she, again, was at the mercy of a Mancini. If there was anything she hated more than not being able to cheat death in the operating room, it was the unfair balance of power given to the rich. And she wasn't about to give up the fight on either front for the sake of Ms. Jenkins. She hoped Matt was ready for the real Georgia tomorrow, not the starry-eyed woman who couldn't compose herself tonight. Tomorrow, the gloves would come off.

Chapter 3

Could there ever be a day where she arrived at morning rounds and have them run smoothly? Georgia had hoped for teaching opportunities, but instead chaos greeted her at Ms. Jenkins' bedside.

"Can we give a milrinone bolus?" she ordered after hearing the nurse summarize the event-filled night.

"Again?" Marion Hammon, a stern, old-school nurse, dared pose the question.

"Yes, again! I'm trying to get her blood pumping here. If you have something better to do, may I suggest you send in a nurse who's willing to save a patient's life?" Georgia had no time to measure her tone before she spoke.

"How much of a bolus do you want, Dr. Laurence?" The charge nurse, Tracey Fisher, stepped up to the bedside and tapped Marion on the shoulder as an order to leave.

"Thank you, Tracey. Fifty micrograms per kilogram bolus over five minutes and a continuous infusion of vasopressin." Georgia reached over to feel Ms. Jenkins' faint jugular pulse.

Tracey left to get the medication and within seconds Marion returned with a self-righteous grin and a pink message slip. "I have a message from the transplant team. Carol says Ms. Jenkins' blood-typing is done and she's Duffy negative, which means that only a person from a small area of Africa can be a heart donor. At this point, a heart transplant is very unlikely, short of a miracle."

Georgia walked Marion to the corner of the room, careful to keep her back to the patient and her voice low, yet spiked with razors. "You are actually smiling. You are standing there with a fucking smile on your face to tell me, in front of my patient, that she has a death sentence. I hope you have a good pension put aside because I think you just ran out of the last ounce of compassion you had left in your nursing career."

Georgia watched Marion's face blanch and then fall, but the show of weakness was soon replaced by a furrowed brow and a puffed chest. Marion marched away and Georgia returned to Ms. Jenkins and held her cold, ashy hand.

The usual battery of intravenous pumps and monitors cluttered the room, but to the right of Ms. Jenkins' bed, on the windowsill, sat a veritable shrine to happiness. It contained myriad get-well cards and a bouquet of cheery balloons. A stuffed zebra held up a handmade sign reading, "I'm praying for a new ticker, Momma! Love, Shawna."

Georgia imagined she would have plastered her own mother's bedside with cards and balloons if only she'd had the chance. Hopefully, her loss would be Shawna's gain. Maybe unlike Georgia, who pursued medicine out of grief and longing, Shawna might one day pursue it because it was what saved her mother.

"You're at the top of the transplant list, Ms. Jenkins. I'm doing everything I can. You just concentrate on your breathing and give that daughter of yours a big hug for me when she drops in later."

Sandra Jenkins' brown eyes held an unspoken plea while a feeble whisper escaped her cyanotic lips. "Thank you."

Georgia gave her hand one more squeeze.

* * *

Matt stood in the doorway. The chaos at Ms. Jenkins' bedside seemed like a full-blown code, except he knew a code hadn't been called. Intermittently encircled by a sea of white lab coats, a woman in her forties lay fighting for every heartbeat. Her grayish complexion screamed transplant candidate. The staff obviously had their hands full trying to get some oxygen to pump through the poor woman.

Dr. Georgia Laurence turned and met his gaze. A warm stirring filled his chest. Her beauty startled him. She was a more refined version of the woman he'd met only briefly a few times so many years ago. She got better with age, like a great wine or a treasured memory.

He wanted to make her smile, to hear her laugh. She needed to unwind a little, she'd always been so driven. There once was a time when her smile filled a room the minute she walked in.

Georgia was probably the only woman Phil had brought home that Matt remembered. She was not only beautiful and intelligent she brought a sauciness his family had never seen. She studied hard and played harder, which was why Phil loved her so much, he was sure, and why Matt barely gave her the time of day back then. He was too busy competing with Phil for his father's attention. He couldn't be bothered to compete with him for women too. Now, he was in a completely different place. He knew better than to compete for his dad's approval and didn't care about breaking some unwritten rule of staying away from your brother's ex. He would love to take Georgia back to her carefree days when she had a joke for every occasion and talked about more than just work.

"Matt. Thanks for coming by this morning." Georgia met him standing just outside room three. "Unfortunately, Ms. Jenkins had a rough night so we didn't do proper rounds. I really wanted you to hear Dr. Carter's summary."

"I think I got the gist of it. She needs a heart transplant yesterday." He followed her as she made her way to the next room.

"You got that right," she said.

He was starting to wonder what the head of cardiac surgery could possibly want from him. Her ebony hair sat high on her head in a ponytail, revealing a deliciously long neck and defined collarbones that dipped into her blue scrubs. He wanted it to be more than his medical opinion. There had to be more to her invitation to rounds this morning. "Was that the expert diagnosis you needed from me?" he asked.

"No. But unfortunately, we're now way behind on our other patients. And I'm in the OR this morning. I'll have to give you the rundown later. Can I meet you for lunch? Around 12:30?"

"Sure. I can introduce you to my caseload. Mildred is faring much better than Ms. Jenkins." He wondered if his groundbreaking research could possibly endear him to someone like Georgia, or if she only gave credence to surgeons like Phil. At what point in his life would he outshine his brother both in medicine and with women like Georgia?

"Well, lucky you. I'll meet you in your office then." She turned and walked off, followed by a trail of lab coat-sporting interns—mama duck and her ducklings.

Why did Georgia want his expertise anyway? Not that he was complaining about her sudden interest in his life's work, but trust was not something Matt bestowed on anyone—especially not on success-hungry surgeons. Phil took care of that a long time ago.

* * *

Georgia listened to Brian run through the discharge protocol for last week's routine triple bypass, but couldn't shake her rage over Marion's comments. This was the last patient to seen on the surgical ward before she went to surgery, and she had to get a handle on her emotions before picking up the scalpel.

She leaned into Joe. "Go ahead and finish up the rounds. I'll meet you in the OR."

"Sure, take your time," he said.

She took the stairs at the back of the ward to buy time. She had no idea what to say. No, strike that. She knew exactly what four-letter words she wanted to say, but none of them would come out professionally enough to be taken seriously. And this was serious.

The stairwell led down to the back of the surgical intensive care unit. The lights were kept dim for the sake of the patients needing their rest, but the old seventies decor with its dark oranges and browns didn't help the dungeon-like atmosphere. She managed to slip into Tracey's office undetected and found the charge nurse standing at an enormous master schedule, lines furrowing her brow.

"I don't envy you your job," Georgia said, trying for a sympathetic smile.

"Middle management. You get it from above and below," Tracey said. "Nobody is ever happy around here. I'm told to cut staff to save money, but at some point, the patient load is too much for the nurses. With the expertise required around here, I can't afford a high turnover, but the good ones will leave if we burn them out." Tracey stood with both hands on her hips, a dry erase marker in one and an eraser in the other.

"You're preaching to the converted." Georgia sat down and leaned back in the chair facing Tracey's desk in the cramped, windowless room.

"I'm sure you're not here to listen to me unload my life's worries on you." Tracey gave up on the schedule and sat at her desk, cocking an eyebrow.

"You're not going to like what I have to say, in light of your last comment, but I'd like to force Marion into retirement, or something." Georgia crossed her arms.

"Wow, she really pissed you off this time. I was planning to talk with her about having to kick her out of the room and get the milrinone bolus myself."

"It's more than that. Yes, she's a good twenty-five years my senior, and yes, she's probably seen more in her career than I have in mine, and for that I owe her some measure of respect. But she's never shown an ounce of respect for my position." She felt the heat rise in her face, so she took a deep breath before she continued. "I swallow my pride and deal with her, and I probably could go on until she used a walker to get around this damned place. But I won't have her take pleasure in announcing that my patient is not a candidate for a heart transplant in front of my patient. I don't give a shit what beef she has with me, but I won't stand by and let her be so unfeeling and uncompassionate to a patient. She stood there and smiled for Christ's sake." Okay, well at least she started off calm and professional, she thought.

"I can't believe she did that," Tracey said. "Well, I can believe that Marion did that, but I can't stand for a nurse on my team to stoop so low."

Tracey turned to a file cabinet behind her desk, pulled out a three-inch-thick file, and plopped it in front of Georgia. "I trust you more than most, Dr. Laurence. You've always gone out of your way to make us all feel like we matter from the orderlies to the housekeepers and the nurses. We've been trying to get rid of Marion for over two years now. Unfortunately, she knows the union handbook as well as you know heart surgery," Tracey said.

At least it wasn't all in Georgia's head then.

"That being said, a complaint from a well-respected cardiac surgeon is exactly the thing that would carry some weight with corporate and against the nurse's union. I can get the proper papers started if you want to drop by and sign them for me after your surgery," Tracey said.

Georgia flipped through the file, feeling her heart sink. One incident report after the other highlighted the human beings this woman had hurt in one way or another. They documented a range of medication errors and complaints from patients and staff in every position: orderlies to nurse managers. But no surgeons.

"Write it up," Georgia said. She stood and turned for the door. "I'll be by before I leave tonight."

She walked down the hall to the OR bay and stood in front of the tiny mirror in her locker. She looked into the eyes of a woman who was sealing the fate of someone's career. Could she do that? She talked a good game, but could she live with herself for being responsible for forcing a nurse to give up her career?

One thought of Ms. Jenkins' pleading brown eyes, and of Marion's smug smile and the hundreds of complaints in her file and she knew that it was Marion herself who had sealed her own fate. Georgia considered it a favor to humanity.

* * *

"Oh, come on, they have sex in the on-call room all the time on *Grey's Anatomy*. Just a quickie. No one will know." Emma Jones never thought she, an upstanding child psychologist, would hear herself whine—practically beg—for sex. But she couldn't get enough of Joe Carter—or his golden hair or smoldering eyes or easy smile—and most of all his chiseled body.

One of her gender-nonconforming patients was admitted to Our Lady of Grace's psych ward on suicide watch, and she'd paged Joe as soon as she finished talking to the psychiatrist taking on the inpatient care.

She and Joe stood entangled in each other's arms in a dim resident's room that was smaller than her walk-in closet.

Room enough for a bed, a side table with a lamp, and a clock. She was sure they could make do with the tight quarters. Heat tingled between her thighs. She needed him bad.

"Babe, there's nothing more I want right now than to have my way with you until you scream, but I'm due in the OR and I can't screw things up for us now," Joe whispered into her neck.

In direct contrast with his words, Joe gave Emma a long, sensual kiss, arcing sparks of desire over her body. He grabbed her butt, pulled her close to his erection, and thrust once through their clothes before leaving the room.

Emma sank down to the bed behind her. He was so worried about his job, so afraid he might have to return to Philadelphia and leave her behind. There must be a way she could help him secure a position in town.

The obvious place to start would be with Georgia. The head of cardiac surgery had to have some pull in securing the next cardiac surgery attending. Maybe it was time to tell her foster sister about this whirlwind romance she'd been hiding. It wasn't like her to bring every guy she dated home to show the family. She did too much of that in her youth and would rather not resurrect that reputation. Clearly, things with Joe were different. Still, she hated using her sister, especially not knowing if he was any good at surgery. But if he was half as skillful with a scalpel as he was in bed, he could perform miracles.

She stood, straightened her blouse, and flattened her hair before cracking the door to be sure no one would see her leave the room. Emma decided to call Georgia's assistant and leave a message to meet her for coffee. She owed Georgia the news of having found the love of her life, at the very least.

Chapter 4

Georgia scrubbed her hands and nails with a Betadine brush and watched Joe Carter through the OR glass as he opened the patient's sternum. A faint tremor rocked her hands as she put down the nailbrush. Her heart followed suit. Why was a routine mitral valve replacement giving her so much stage fright?

Georgia had done or assisted on at least six hundred of them in her career. So, why the nerves? Because she just decided to end someone's career? No, because Ms. Jenkins was the last to be blessed with her surgical skill on a mitral valve, and she'd had no miracles to offer her. She was failing Sandra Jenkins and her daughter. This wasn't stage fright. She'd lost patients before. This was about another motherless child.

After a long rinse, Georgia lifted her hands and waited for the automatic door to slide open. The circulating nurse met her immediately with a pair of size seven sterile gloves, followed by a sterile gown. The tremor returned. There was no way she could operate like this. The head of cardiac surgery, the youngest doctor, and the first woman to ever hold that title in the history of Our Lady of Grace, and she dared not hold a scalpel.

"How does it look there, Joe?" Georgia asked.

"Great, this one's a piece of cake." Joe smiled with his eyes above his surgical mask.

A piece of cake? Surely, she could handle a piece of cake. She clasped her hands in front of her chest in order to preserve the sterile field, also to hide the tremor. Her heart hitched up a few beats per minute again.

She couldn't do it.

She had no choice.

"Good. I'll just stand here and watch you do all the work for a change." She took a few deep breaths to see if she could shake the feeling.

"Seriously? I'm flying solo on this one?" Joe's eyes squinted from an even wider smile.

"We'll see how far you can take it on your own," she said.

"Aw man, thanks. You know, this is just what I need, this kind of experience, if I'm going to get the only attending position open next year. I've done my homework and short of returning to Philadelphia, this place is my only hope with all the competition out there. Otherwise, I'd have to move. And I really don't want to go back to Philly."

"Why's that? I thought you only-sons liked to be near your mamas?" Georgia waited for a smartass comeback but was denied.

"I met The One, Dr. L." Joe looked up, holding his Kelly clamp in the air and waited for her reply. None came, so he continued, waving the clamp as he spoke. "I'm even thinking of how I can save up some extra money for a ring."

"How about you put those instruments back into Mrs. Reynold's heart there, lover boy, and we'll talk about the wife material later, okay?" A glance up at the heart monitor assured Georgia's nerves. Time and the surgery ticked along smoothly.

"You never did tell me how things went with Dr. Mancini and the stem cell research." Joe peeked over his surgical glasses.

"Yeah, well, we can talk about that later, too, but it looks like a no-go. Timing is all off." Georgia watched and admired Joe's astuteness in his every move.

"I was afraid of that. So, the lunch date I heard you set earlier, is that business or pleasure?"

"It's not a date," she said, giving him a look that dared him to proceed with that line of conversation.

The circulating nurse chirped up. "You have a page, Dr. Laurence. Want me to dial for you?"

"Yes, please," she said.

Georgia walked over to the phone and leaned her ear in with her hands still clamped to her front. The surgical ICU was having a hard time keeping Ms. Jenkins' electrolytes balanced. She gave a verbal order for more oral potassium because her patient couldn't take more IV fluids. She asked about the other patients in the unit and had to wait for them to grab the other nurse and then updated a few more orders.

She had barely finished her sentence when the anesthetist started yelling. "Whoa, holy deceleration, Batman! We're coding here."

"What the hell is going on? I turned my back for five fucking minutes, Joe." Georgia rushed back to the table.

"Injecting atropine," the anesthetist announced, ignoring Georgia's outburst. He'd heard it all before.

"I was getting ready to close her up. Did I nick her left ventricle?"

"Heart rate is coming up," a nurse announced.

"How do you nick a ventricle when closing up? Get out of the way and let me finish." Georgia's shakes were gone.

When it came right down to it, her need to help and her knowledge of surgery overrode a bit of shaken self-confidence. Besides, Mrs. Reynolds' heart was in great condition, nothing like Ms. Jenkins. Her hands moved like those of a well-trained pianist.

"There," she said. "The beautiful click of a mechanical valve. I'm sorry for yelling at you, bud, and I don't see any nicks or bleeding anywhere. You did fine, Joe. Must have been a fluke." She continued to close up the chest wound.

"It won't happen again, Dr. Laurence," Joe said flatly.

"Don't give me that Dr. Laurence crap. I'm hungry, so you go write up the post-op orders and don't forget this is a metallic valve and we don't want blood clots on it, right?"

"Oh, you just want to rush off for that not-a-date of yours?" Joe headed to the door, pulling off his surgical gloves.

"Shut up. I didn't say I forgave you yet." Not that there was anything to forgive. Decelerations happened all the time in surgery, and she was the one with the self-confidence issue today.

"I love you too." Joe blew her a kiss and she winked at him. She sure did hope he made it past all the others to become the attending. She appreciated his quick mind.

* * *

Matt opened the door to the animal lab. "Let me show you where my patient is kept." He led the way down the hall, inhaling Georgia's woodsy scent as they walked.

"Here's our little Mildred, up and about second-day post-op." He walked her over to a pen in the corner of the large room.

After spending time that morning in the intensive care unit, he appreciated the quiet of his animal lab. Even though they used very similar machines and procedures and were surrounded by animals, he took pride in how his workplace was less of a zoo than Georgia's. Mildred's pen was kept very clean, both to help in her healing and because Matt saw no reason for this place to smell like a barn.

"Wow. This is quite the setup. What are your plans for reassessment?"

"Cell growth usually doubles in three-and-a-half days. We'll do the whole battery of tests on her a week post-op. But I can already see a change in her," he boasted.

"This is very promising stuff." Georgia scratched the

pig's head. Matt handed her an apple slice from the daily rations on the counter. She leaned over the pen, and Mildred let out a snort as she nuzzled the hand that fed her.

"I should show you the real magic. The cells are kept in the fridge in the next room. You have no idea how thrilled I am to be part of this research," he said. The part he didn't say aloud was that this research would guarantee him an exceptional career and legacy of his own outside of the shadow of his father and brother. His field would get the respect it deserved in the medical community, and he might even gain the recognition he deserved from his family.

"Why does research always take so long?" Georgia asked. "You saw Ms. Jenkins. She needs these cells now."

Matt twisted the head on his stethoscope. Why did every surgeon always ask that same question? He didn't invent the scientific method.

She turned her back to him, washing pig saliva from her hands in the sink. "Those cells are the answer for a woman to be able to see her daughter graduate from high school, backpack around Europe, and follow her dreams one day. I can't let her down, Matt. She needs me. She needs us to cure her of this horrible defective heart. I wish we could speed up the clinical trial results and use Ms. Jenkins as our first human recipient."

"It's just not the right time," he led the way into the next room.

"Can we make it the right time? Move the schedule up a bit?'

"No. We'd be jeopardizing the credibility of the research I want to see get published and adopted by the medical community," he said. "This should be used to help millions of patients long into the future. Not to mention what all that will do for my career."

"I know," she said. He noticed her nostrils flare slightly

as she inhaled. "Unfortunately, at this point, it would be the only thing that could save Ms. Jenkins."

No way was this woman, the head of cardiac surgery, standing there asking him to break protocol. She was testing his moral code, his ethical backbone. That was it. The board of directors must be checking in on him and his standards by using the most gorgeous woman in the hospital to try to sway him. He'd just have to prove himself.

"Absolutely and unequivocally, no," he said. "It's not going to happen Dr. Laurence."

Why couldn't she have come to his office to ask him to sleep with her? That, he'd have considered. But there was no way he'd throw away the possibilities for the future of medicine under a bus for her.

* * *

Georgia walked into the coffee shop down the road from the hospital. The one with the good coffee, not the watered-down swill they sold in the cafeteria. The aroma of freshly ground coffee beans filled the cafe and she knew that part of her coffee addiction was the ritual of going to the coffee shop and drinking in the sights, smells, and sounds in there. She saw Emma cradling a steaming cup and waved as she lined up to order.

After a short wait, Georgia headed to the table with a large vanilla latte. "How's life? You've been remarkably unavailable for the last two months."

"Life is fan-fucking-tastic! I think I'm in love," Emma said.

"Whoa. Since when?" Georgia never thought she'd hear any of those words come out of Emma's mouth.

"I met him at a bar a few months ago."

"Who the hell are you and where did you put my

Emma? First, you don't go to bars and second, you certainly don't pick men up there." Georgia inhaled the scent of her coffee before taking the first sip.

Emma laughed. "Oh, it's not like that," she said. "It was a martini bar with a bunch of old stiffs from the American Psychology Association. I drank soda with lime. He was there with two married couples, and we were both bored out of our minds. He came over and we started to chat. Next thing I know I've seen him almost every single day since." Emma absolutely beamed.

"What does he do?"

"He's a doctor," Emma replied.

"That's elusive. What kind of doctor? Where does he work?" Georgia had to admit she felt some relief knowing it was someone she could easily find out more about.

"What is this, twenty questions? A surgeon."

"You are my Emma. Whoever wants to date you has to meet my approval," Georgia said with a smile.

They'd really lucked out, both of them, with the best foster family. Tom and Vicki had sought the best treatments for Emma's ADHD, which had been a result, so they were told, of having addicts for biological parents. Georgia looked at Emma, a successful child psychologist, and herself, orphaned at twelve and now head of cardiac surgery, as anomalies—they'd been fortunate beyond measure.

Georgia, however, didn't allow Tom and Vicki to help her out as much as they would have liked. A pre-teen losing her mother is a perfect breeding ground for anger and independence. Fool that she was, she split at the age of sixteen, sure she knew better than everyone else. And who's to say if she did or didn't. She eventually got everything she'd ever wanted in life. The struggle was not easy, but she was no shrinking violet in the face of hard work. But Tom and Vicki patiently stood by and maintained the family bonds somehow. They continued to host the family for Sunday brunch as often as the kids were off work.

Maybe she'd go see Tom and Vicki for Sunday brunch. She owed them that much, she thought, flipping over her phone.

* * *

After the third time Georgia checked her smartphone, Emma covered it with her hand. Emma was supposed to be the antsy one, and it was Georgia who was so easily distracted.

"What's going on?" Emma asked.

"I'm losing it, Emma. I have a patient who's hanging on with the tips of her fingernails. She's as good as dead. And I've got nothing. She needs a new heart and her blood type is too rare. Then I find out the most gorgeous man to ever hold a petri dish could save her life, and he's not even remotely interested in breaking protocol for me."

"What are you talking about?" Emma held Georgia's hand on the table between them.

"Matt Mancini's stem cell clinical trial is the only hope I have of saving this woman. She's a single mother. If she dies, what's going to happen to her daughter? She's only thirteen. Not a whole lot of kids luck out with foster parents like Tom and Vicki. She could end up on the streets."

"Georgie, this is not your mother, and the daughter will not be on the streets. You're making it personal," Emma warned. "You haven't changed at all from the girl who'd usher a spider out the door instead of killing it."

"It is personal," Georgia said. "It's my career on the line. I got the shakes in the OR today. My faith is slipping."

Georgia drew circles in the condensation from her coffee cup. Emma had known her for almost twenty years now, and though most of the world saw Georgia as a tough-as-nails surgeon, she knew her tender, caring, and vulnerable side all too well. But still, what was it with these career-driven surgeons?

"You're a brilliant woman and a skillful surgeon, but you can't expect to fix everyone that comes across your operating room table," Emma said. "Don't you think that makes you a little too self-important? You've lost patients before, right?"

"This gig's all I've got," Georgia said into her coffee.

"Maybe you need a couple of weeks off work to put things into perspective. A nice sandy beach and a drink with an umbrella in it."

"Perspective. Maybe I can ask Matt to ask around in the research community for something else I can use. It's worth a shot. I have nothing of my own to offer."

Emma had always admired Georgia's strength and dedication to heart health. She took care of herself by jogging every day after she moved out of home, while Emma ingested every poison from cocaine to cola, giving their foster parents too many sleepless nights. Her own line of work was an attempt at saving kids from her mistakes, she couldn't fault Georgia for her ambition.

"Okay, well maybe you need to think about something else. Let's talk about me and my hottie," Emma said.

"Oh, gag. You sound like you're fifteen!"

"I have never had so much sex in my life, and I can't get enough!" That was a guaranteed laugh from Georgia. And it worked.

"Who is this sex-crazed surgeon? Do I know him?"

"Dr. Joseph Carter." Emma noticed the heat rise to her cheeks as she said his name. She certainly felt like she was fifteen again.

"Joe? My chief resident? Really? The best sex you've ever had?" Georgia crinkled her nose as if she'd just pictured their parents having sex.

"Up until two weeks ago when he said he's in love with me. Now he's in the hospital non-stop trying to secure the only attending position this year."

"You're the 'wife material'?" Georgia's eyes widened.

"Is that what he called me?"

"No, no, that's what I called you. He called you 'The One.'"

That was an announcement Emma wasn't prepared to hear. She was having a great time with this guy and she did care for him, maybe even loved him. But marriage? "The One"? She was too busy enjoying all the physical attention and natural high lately to think about a future with him. But, if it meant a lifetime of being in bed with him, she'd have to think about it, and she'd have to consider having kids of her own one day. What would that mean to her career? Her thoughts bounced all over the place and she started to bounce her leg under the table.

"You're the big cheese over there in cardiac surgery, any chance you can make sure he gets the job, so I can get my boyfriend to relax a bit?"

"What the fuck, Emma?" Georgia laughed, "This isn't high school. I'm not about to make someone attending so you can get laid. Have you been taking your medication lately?"

Emma felt that flippant comment like a slap in the face. "I am taking my medication. In fact, I just upped the dose recently. Not that it's any of your business." She hadn't felt this alive in a long time—a little too alive. She'd noticed a few of her impulses creeping up on her but didn't have a chance to see her doctor about it. She must remember to do that.

"Yeah, well, you are my business. Always. Listen, as much as I'd really love to not hear about your sex life, I've got to get back. Let's go visit Tom and Vicki on Sunday. I need a family moment, and by the sounds of things, so do you."

"Okay, sure." Sunday was years away. She needed to plan a special night for Joe. Tonight was his night off and she was going to make sure there was no sleeping involved.

Chapter 5

Matt scratched the top of the pig's prickly head. "Today's the day we see if we have the next cure for heart disease on our hands, Mildred."

He nodded to Ken Liu, his lab assistant, who turned on the ultrasound monitor. Matt squeezed blue jelly onto Mildred's chest and spread it with the ultrasound wand in search of her left ventricle. He certainly hadn't thought he'd be poking around in pigs for a living, but when research became his undying passion, working with animals became part of the process.

"One step closer to history being made. Can you believe it, Ken?" Matt said. If the procedure worked, and Mildred's heart tissue repaired itself after they'd injected the myocardial stem cells, heart disease treatment would be a whole new ball game.

"Not to mention that we'll have a small fortune and very prestigious careers ahead of us," Ken said, smiling.

Matt and Ken became friends after working so closely on this project over the last few years. When he noticed that Ken rode his bike to work in all four seasons, Matt introduced him to cyclocross. This study getting published would turn Ken's whole life around and would help pay back his immigrant parents for all their sacrifices. Those thoughts occupied just a tiny bit smaller place in Matt's mind than the benevolence of saving lives. With a twinge of guilt, he allowed himself the indulgence of yearning for the long-awaited recognition that came with making medical history. The kind of recognition that showed he was as good as his brother, Phil.

From the time Phillip came out of the womb, he had made everything a competition, from learning to tie their shoes, to sculpting clay in kindergarten, to every report card. But that wasn't anything more than most sibling rivalries. No, Phil clearly became Dad's special project after middle-school when Phil almost drowned in a sailing accident. The whole family blamed Matt for not stopping Phil from taking the boat out alone. No one would hear that there was nothing Matt could have done to stop Phil. From that moment on Phil did no wrong.

Phil had followed in their dad's footsteps to become a phenomenal orthopedic surgeon. Matt was much happier actually finding cures rather than playing with hammers and screws and glue and brute force replacing hips and knees. But that was him. Phil and Dad never acknowledged the nobility of medical research in the biochemistry field. Hopefully curing heart disease would be a step in that direction.

"Yeah, well, we have to share some of the glory with the team in California too, you know—would you look at that?" Matt said, pointing to the ultrasound screen.

"What?" Ken leaned in.

"A beautiful, strong, contracting heart. I want a cardiac index now. Let's prep her for a cardiac catheter, Ken."

"You're going to cath the pig now? I thought we were waiting another week."

"I've been thinking we could speed things up a bit. She has our success in her left ventricle. I want all the proof I can get." Matt printed all the images from the scanner.

Not to mention that, thanks to Georgia and Ms. Jenkins, he was starting to see the need for success from a patient care point of view. He wasn't heartless. He knew all too well how hard death could be on those who love them.

Ken got the equipment out of the cart in the hall while Matt adjusted the sedation pump. "Okay, Mildred. You relax, this is a simple procedure," Matt said. "We're all counting on you trotting away happy and healthy. I have an ear of corn with your name on it, sweetheart."

"Do you always talk to sedated lab animals as if they'll actually do what you tell them to?" Ken said, snickering.

"Yep. You insert the heart catheter while I go check something in my office." Matt started to leave but added, "See, I can give instructions to alert lab assistants too."

Matt walked down the hall to his office where he quickly signed into his desktop to add a note to Mildred's file and checked his e-mail, but Bruce Childs hadn't replied. He'd been thinking of Georgia and her obvious attachment to Ms. Jenkins all day. He hoped to contact a colleague who might have something to help Ms. Jenkins until she could get a new heart.

He left his desk and poked his head in Judy's office. "Can you get Dr. Bruce Childs at John Hopkins for me? Tell him I need to talk to him ASAP. I need a favor."

"Sure thing, Dr. Mancini," she said. "When you get a chance, I have some papers from California for you to sign off on. They still haven't sent this quarter's money and the lab staff is getting a little hungry for their paychecks."

"Oh, for crying out loud. Transfer the money from my personal contributions fund for now. I'll sign the papers before I leave tonight." He ran his fingers through his hair in utter frustration. Same song and dance every time he dealt with California's lab director.

He headed to the lab, hoping a nice cardiac index would erase some of the tension California's lack of funding placed in his shoulders. They were consistently late with funding and it wasn't the first time Matt had to bail them out with his own money. It was the curse of the Mancini family name. Everyone knew them as the Kardashians of medicine and thought they sweated dollar bills. They took advantage of the family's deep pockets as much as they could. But he had something much more valuable than money in his lab refrigerator because no one could put a price tag on life.

There was something about Georgia's concern for her patient that knocked old memories out of the cobwebs of his mind. More than seven years ago he had lost the love of his life to ovarian cancer. By the time it was found, Christine was on her deathbed. He had proposed, even though they were both so young. He had fully intended to make her his wife and damned if he would let cancer get in the way. But it had. Losing Christine had been such a blow, he purposefully avoided cancer research. For years, the mere mention of ovarian cancer shredded his soul. With his attention squarely focused on his stem cells, he hadn't thought of Christine in months.

To reassure himself of the preciousness of his medical miracle, Matt stopped by the room containing the genetic reprogramming medium. He liked to take the syringes and tumble them a few times a day, admiring the fact that within that bit of serum were tiny building block cells that could multiply and heal. He opened the refrigerator. Panic rose in his throat. Only three syringes stood in the metal tray.

One was missing.

His whole body went cold. He closed the refrigerator and leaned on it. No one knew where the stem cells were kept except for his lab assistants. And Georgia.

His lab assistants wanted this clinical trial to be successful as much as he did. They'd all toiled over this study near and far for the last seven years. They'd all get publishing rights. They'd all have secure careers and futures. No one on his staff would mess around with the cells. Georgia. Was she desperate enough? Was she testing his ethics or was she suggesting breaking the law and breaking protocol?

Could he have been swayed by her stunning smile to

lead her right to where the cells were kept? He'd practically given her a crash course in stem cell implantation. And here he was pulling in favors to help her out.

As if on cue, Judy called out from down the hall: "Dr. Mancini, I have Dr. Childs on line one for you."

There was no way he was remotely calm enough to talk to Bruce right now, besides the fact that the rage building in his head wouldn't allow him to ask for a favor for Georgia's sake. He went into the hallway and yelled down to Judy. "Tell him I'll call him tomorrow."

"But you said ASAP! I pulled him out of the OR," she yelled back.

"Tomorrow!" His fury came through louder than he intended.

Matt strode into the lab room where Ken was recording Mildred's numbers.

"Looks great over here, Matt."

"Did you move a batch of stem cells out of the fridge?" Matt asked.

"No, why the hell would I do that?" Ken turned to face his boss.

Matt paced the length of the pig's stretcher. The situation had to be contained before anyone found out. "This is between you and me. A syringe is missing," Matt said. "I might have an idea of where it went, but you have to keep this quiet. Any wind of stem cells gone astray can cost us this trial. Do you hear me? This is a big deal. I need to find those cells or whoever took them. Right now. You take care of Mildred for me and keep your mouth shut."

"I will. I'll keep my eyes on the rest of them too," Ken reassured him.

"Thanks." Matt left, making his way to the elevators.

Matt hoped he was wrong about who took the cells. He could think of others out there who would want to jeopardize his research. Everyone knew the debate over stem cell research. When the scientists started using embryonic cells and the extreme-right media made certain to humanize those tiny cells, the amount of shit that hit the fan in his field of work could fertilize every crop in North America. Now that they used human skin cells the debate stayed at a low hum, but he never knew when the next zealot would show up and question his work.

But it had been months since he last received hate mail. That left one person to ask.

* * *

Georgia returned to the hospital refreshed and caffeinated. Though now, in addition to being worried about helping Ms. Jenkins, she worried about Emma's state of mind. Stopping her meds was the most reckless thing she'd done in over a decade. And Georgia didn't know how she felt about Joe sleeping with her foster sister. How was she even going to look him in the eye now? At some point, though, she was going to have to get Emma to tell him the truth about her neurodiversity. She didn't have time to formulate a plan as the overhead pager rang code blue in surgical intensive care, bed four, seconds after she walked through the hospital doors. That was Mrs. Reynolds, her routine mitral valve from this morning.

Georgia sprinted through the lobby and down the stairs, rushing through the double doors to the surgical intensive care unit.

"What the fuck is going on?" she said.

Marion stood between the bed and the crash cart. What on Earth was she doing caring for one of Georgia's patients?

"She's in tamponade. We started the routine blood thinners and less than half an hour later she started to code," Marion said.

Fluid had accumulated in the sac around the heart and it couldn't pump. Solution number one: Get rid of the fluid, and then get rid of Marion.

"Where's the chest tube box? Did someone check for a clot?" Georgia asked.

Marion gestured across the room. "Not yet, it's over there. You can check it."

Georgia had intended for Marion to check it. Imagine: being told what to do while coding her own patient. If Georgia had claws and fangs, she'd be showing them right now.

"Where's Tracey?" Georgia made no effort to conceal her anger in her question.

"She's gone to a board meeting. Donna's in charge for the rest of the afternoon." Finally, Marion's somber eyes showed some fear that she might be told to leave again.

Georgia's eyes followed the yellow rubber tube that led from Mrs. Reynolds' chest to a white calibrated box hanging off the bed's side rails.

"Shit! It's filling up. She's bleeding to death. Give me a pericardiocentesis tray, now." She whipped on a pair of latex gloves. To hell with the sterility of the operating room, she'd worry about antibiotics if her patient had an ounce of blood left in her by day's end.

To Georgia's relief, another younger nurse came in with the tray and other supplies placing them on the wheeled table. Georgia opened the tray and grabbed a syringe while feeling for the fifth intercostal space on Mrs. Reynolds' bare chest. Found it. She swiped the skin with iodine and poked through the now-orange flesh with the syringe. Bright red blood filled the barrel. As with any code, an army of nurses, a respiratory therapist, and porters flocked into the room to await her orders.

"Give me the clips remover, I'm going to open her chest

to see if I can stop the bleed," Georgia ordered no one in particular.

No one questioned her this time. The nurses were two steps ahead of her every need. In seconds, she was wearing a sterile gown, mask, and eye shield, and holding the clips remover.

The staples came out like they were in butter. The metal bindings holding the sternum together took a bit more force to twist off. Finally, she reached the pericardial sac bulging with blood.

"I hope someone has had the bright idea to stop the heparin drip?" Georgia asked.

"I did, Dr. Laurence," Donna said from the head of the bed.

"I'll take six abdominal pads, please, and hook up the suction. Get some blood hung stat and put the saline on the pump full tilt." Georgia's orders automatically fired out.

She blotted her way to the heart tissue and gave it a few massaging strokes to reperfuse Mrs. Reynolds' body. It was apparent where all the blood was coming from—with every manual contraction, blood spurted into the air from a puncture wound in the left ventricle. Where in the hell did a hole that size come from?

"I need a 1.0 silk suture," Georgia called out.

Donna opened the suture kit on the table in front of Georgia and let the suture fall out of its packaging on the sterile field. She also placed her hand on Georgia's shoulder. "Looks like an awful lot of blood loss, Dr. Laurence."

Georgia closed the hole in seconds and manually pumped the heart again. But it had little effect. She pulled back from her view of the open chest and the feeble wavelengths on the heart monitor to see a bloodbath in the intensive care cubicle. Game over.

She stopped pumping the heart and watched the flat

lines string along the monitor. Mrs. Reynolds' heart lay like a deflated balloon in front of her.

"Time of death 14:08," Georgia said.

A warm, slimy feeling bathed her toes. When she removed her gloves and gown she noticed the blood smeared across her legs. Her shoes were crimson. The sight of blood inside a patient never bothered her, but wearing her patient's lifeforce... the intimacy of it turned her stomach.

"Is the family around?" Georgia asked Donna.

"They left for the afternoon. We'll have to call them in."

"Call them and page Dr. Carter to talk to them. I'm heading to the locker room to shower. I'll be back to chart in fifteen minutes." Georgia pulled off her shoes and put on the blue OR slippers Donna had provided.

"Do you want HIV and hepatitis tests done, doctor?" Donna asked in a whisper.

"Only on the patient's blood. I'll let you know if I find any open wounds on my feet. I should be fine," Georgia said, the words sounding, but not feeling, true.

It was a short trip across the hall to the locker rooms, and somehow she bumped into the one person she didn't want to see while covered in blood from a patient she'd just lost.

Matt practically ran the length of the hall between them. "Can we speak in private?" he said, not commenting on the state of her.

"Now is really not a good time for me, Matt."

"Now." The look of utter fury on Matt's face as he said it told her to lead the way to the nearest storage room.

"I'm getting the sense you're having a bad day too," she said, her temper threatening to boil over. "Did you have a pig bleed all over your Prada shoes?"

"I'm not in a laughing mood," he said. "You wouldn't

happen to know where a syringe of stem cells has run off to, would you?"

"What are you talking about?" She crossed her arms.

"A syringe full of stem cells went missing from my lab today," he said. Georgia could see a vein bulging at his temple. "You're the only one, besides my staff, who knows my lab setup. You're the one with the dying patient. Do you know anything about where those cells are?"

"Oh my God. You're really going to stand there and accuse me, the head of cardiac surgery, of stealing your stem cells?" Georgia eyed the rack of catheters behind Matt and resisted the temptation to shove the largest one into his bladder.

"You're desperate enough to do it, Georgia," he said. "You even had me convinced to push up Mildred's testing and call in favors to find some kind of help for Ms. Jenkins to survive long enough to be our first human trial. I was bending over backward for you, but apparently, you were in too much of a rush."

"Listen, Dr. Mancini, I didn't take your fucking cells," she said. "I have no clue where they are. I'm going to pretend that you didn't accuse me of breaking the law and every ethical code that I stand for. Now get out of my way. I've just had a patient bleed to death all over me, so I'm going to take a shower, and I sincerely hope I won't see your face around my end of the hospital for a very long time."

* * *

Georgia stood under the scalding stream of water and thought long and hard. She was beyond pissed that Matt accused her of stealing his stem cells. She'd hoped that inviting Matt to meet Ms. Jenkins might have helped push up the first human trial, but she would never steal the cells. As much as Matt's accusations hurt, she still liked him, so the awful things he thought about her made her want to bathe in

Betadine. The metallic smell of Mrs. Reynolds' blood mixed with the sweet smell of her body wash turned her stomach.

She tried to force Matt out of her thoughts and in popped Emma, wanting her to hire Joe. Who, up until today, she thought could walk on water, but she had to wonder about the hole in the heart he'd described as a possible nick during the operation. How could he nick the heart with a suture needle? She wouldn't have missed that. Would she? Then there was the bleeding. She hadn't found anything wrong with the heart during the operation. But something made Mrs. Reynolds bleed to death, and she would wear that mistake. A life was lost and it was her fault.

And to top it off, if those cells really were missing and were in the wrong hands, Matt could lose all the years and effort he spent on that clinical trial. She knew the benefits of that trial and Ms. Jenkins needed its benefits. He couldn't go to the police with a missing cells report. Not yet. That would completely taint his good standing with this research. It would permanently be a stain on the history of the study. He had to find them himself. And she was more than a little curious about Matt calling in favors that could save Ms. Jenkins. Maybe she'd made a dent in his compassion after all.

She turned the water off and reached for a towel. Her feet were fine, not a scratch anywhere on them, so no blood tests required.

She figured she should be the one to talk to Mrs. Reynolds' family, not Joe. It wouldn't be fair to him since she'd declared there had been no nick in the OR this morning. Then she had to convince Matt she had nothing to do with the missing stem cells.

* * *

Georgia walked into the family lounge, which wasn't much more than four walls and two couches. Nancy

Reynolds' now-widower husband and their adult daughter sat on one couch holding hands in their laps. Each face wore pure fear. Getting called into the hospital for an update without seeing their loved one didn't bode well.

"We met a couple of weeks ago in my office, I'm Dr. Georgia Laurence." She extended her hand for a shake.

"Why were we called back?" Mr. Reynolds said. "The nurses said Nancy would be sleeping for another couple of hours."

"Mr. Reynolds, there's been a terribly unfortunate event, and Nancy died a short while ago." Georgia gently got straight to the point. No use in prolonging their stress to avoid her own discomfort.

The daughter melted into a puddle of sobs in her father's lap sending Mr. Reynolds over the edge. His face turned crimson in a heartbeat.

"What happened?" he demanded.

"We aren't exactly sure at this point," Georgia said. "But your wife lost a lot of blood after surgery. It seems she had a puncture in her heart and the blood thinners to prevent clots from forming on her metal valve also stopped the puncture wound from closing."

"Your resident said the risks were mostly from the anesthetic or infection or blood clots. He never talked about bleeding to death," said Mr. Reynolds, spit pooling at the corners of his mouth. "That's what you're saying, right? That she bled to death from a puncture wound? Where did that come from, your complete and utter incompetence?"

Georgia was at a loss. She should have had Joe with her. He was the one who would have explained the risks of surgery, that's always the chief resident's job, and bleeding is always a risk with any surgery. Not necessarily from a huge puncture wound in the heart, though.

"You have every right to be angry and frustrated," she

finally said. "I didn't see a puncture on the heart at the time of closing, but there was one at the time of resuscitation. With your permission, I would like to order an autopsy to clarify what went wrong."

"Oh, I want an autopsy for sure. I want your ass in a sling, Dr. Laurence." Mr. Reynolds was shouting now. "You killed my wife. We were going on a cruise around the world this summer. We worked our whole lives to spend our retirement together and you stole her right out from under me. I'll see that you lose everything. The way I just did. You'll pay with your medical license. That's a promise."

"Dad, settle down," his daughter pleaded with a tear-stained face. "Getting mad isn't going to bring Mom back."

Calm on the outside, shaken on the inside, Georgia stood and took the last word with all the dignity she could muster. "I'll contact you personally as soon as I have the autopsy report."

Chapter 6

On her way out of the family lounge, Georgia grabbed Tracey at the door to her office.

"You need to get Donna and both of you go see the Reynolds family in the family lounge. Mrs. Reynolds bled out. I'm ordering an autopsy."

"Oh, my that's horrible. Geez, your day just keeps getting better and better. Thank God it's Friday." Tracey offered a sympathetic pat on Georgia's shoulder.

Somehow, Georgia didn't think the weekend would make much of a difference.

"Be careful, Mr. Reynolds is deep in the anger phase of grief," she said.

Georgia sat at the nursing station, wrote up the autopsy order and filled in the death certificate. She replayed the surgery in her mind, rewinding to the part where she was paged to the phone and then returned to a decelerating heart. Joe had to be right. He had to have done something for the heart to react that way.

She'd seen nothing on the heart tissue, and yet the hole in the left ventricle, the one pissing blood everywhere, would have been hard to miss. Why hadn't she seen anything?

"Where the hell is Joe Carter?" Georgia asked as a ward clerk passed. She really needed him to help her figure out what happened to Mrs. Reynolds.

"He went into surgery with Dr. Williams. Emergency bypass of a cardiac cath gone bad. We're expecting them out in about an hour. Going to bed one."

"Thanks." She'd meant it rhetorically, but that ward clerk

was obviously the person to ask if anyone wanted to know who had the meatloaf special for lunch.

Georgia peeked in on Ms. Jenkins and found her daughter, Shawna, at the bedside holding her hand.

"My mom hasn't been feeling very well today," Shawna said. The girl's big, dark brown eyes pleaded for help.

"I know, honey," Georgia said, lowering herself beside Shawna. "I've been monitoring her and giving her everything I possibly can to help her out."

"Any news on the transplant?"

"Not yet. We're waiting for the right donor to show up."

"It's kind of gross that somebody has to die for my mom to live." Shawna crinkled her nose.

"Don't think about it that way, Shawna," Georgia said. "We have no control over when people die, and they die whether or not your mom needs a transplant." Georgia saw how hard Sandra Jenkins had worked to raise a healthy child. Shawna's skin glowed, her neatly braided hair shone, and her half-hearted smile showed the results of a healthy diet and good oral hygiene. The school uniform and heavy book bag would be enough to hint at her level of intelligence, but her thoughtful and articulate conversation surpassed any expectations. Georgia saw so much potential in Shawna, a tender seedling taking root in an open field.

"How are things at home, Shawna?"

"The social worker's been snooping around our place again, looking for Aunt Jackie. I've had to lie a lot and say that she's at work when the only work she's doing is looking for more drugs and booze," Shawna said with a sigh.

"Are you okay with money and groceries and stuff?"

"Yeah, Mom gave me all her bank cards, passwords, and PIN numbers. I've been able to pay the bills and do everything online, so nobody asks why my mom looks like she's thirteen all of a sudden."

Georgia leaned in and hugged Shawna. "Your mom has every reason to be proud of you. You go get a healthy supper and some rest. I'm going to bug a very smart friend of mine to see if he can help find something else to make your mom feel better until a heart comes along."

Georgia was reminded of her resolve to go beg Matt for help—again. On her way to the elevator, her phone buzzed a text. It was the hospital CEO, Gregory Douglas, asking for a few words about Mrs. Reynolds.

"Oh, for Christ's sake!" Instead of heading to the research wing, she went to her office to make the call.

When she walked through her office anteroom, her assistant stood, but Georgia lifted her hand and Diane sat right back down. Diane's work—and her four cats—were her whole life, which made her the best assistant Georgia had ever had. She listened, really listened, and didn't take Georgia's moods seriously, which made their relationship run like a well-oiled machine.

She threw herself into her high-back leather chair and ran her hands over her face.

"What a fucking mess," she said to no one.

She'd been referring to her present situation, but she could just as easily have been talking about her desk. Ms. Jenkins' case had been her top priority and her administrative duties were suffering as a result. She had at least a week's worth of paperwork to sift through. She'd better text the dog walker to check on Gus because she would be spending the better part of the night catching up. But she knew she needed to call Dr. Douglas.

She picked up her phone and dialed her boss. He answered on the first ring and she replied, "What's up, Greg?"

"A very angry Mr. Reynolds left my office a minute ago promising to spend all of his retirement money on a lawyer until you lose your license. Should I be calling our lawyers about this one?"

"Yup," she said.

"What do you mean, 'yup'? How can you be so glib? What happened to Nancy Reynolds?"

"I don't know," Georgia said. She walked him through everything that had happened.

"So, it was human error?"

"That and I think Mr. Reynolds is especially pissed that no one told him one of the risks of surgery is bleeding to death," she said. "I wasn't there when he signed the consent, so I can't say."

"Has your chief resident had these issues before? It's Joe Carter, right?"

"Joe is the best I've worked with in years. I don't know what's going on. He mentioned a personal issue this morning. I'll have a talk with him tonight." She wondered if this love affair between Emma and Joe was getting them both in over their heads. You'd think neither one of them had ever had a relationship before.

"Anything else you want me to tell the lawyers and the malpractice insurance adjusters?" Dr. Douglas asked.

"You can tell them I ordered an autopsy," she said. "Hopefully, we'll know what the hell really happened."

"Okay, well, it being Friday and all, I suggest you and Dr. Carter stay out of the OR for a couple of days until the dust settles. I'll get Dr. Habibi to do your scheduled surgeries on Monday. No emergency surgeries over the weekend."

"What?" she said. "You're not seriously pulling me off duty?" This had never happened before.

"I'm just keeping you out of the OR until we receive the autopsy results," he said. "I can't afford the wrath of the board if you're found at fault and I still let you operate."

"Thanks for the vote of confidence there, Greg."

"You said yourself you have no idea what happened. Let's find out. You deserve a break anyway," he said. "Besides, you're way behind on your paperwork. This will give you a chance to catch up."

What, did he have a camera in her office?

"Yeah, yeah, your benevolence is overwhelming, Greg. I'll be in your office Monday morning with the autopsy report in hand."

She hung up and flipped the bird to the receiver, hoping he did have a camera on her. She pulled out her cell and called her foster mother. At this point, what she really needed was a spreadsheet and action plan for all the parts of her life that were falling apart. Vicki's home cooking would have to suffice.

"Hey, Vick, I miss you."

"We miss you too, Georgie. Nice to hear from you. It's been a while." Vicki's gentle tone was a balm.

"Too long. Listen, I saw Emma today and she seems awfully off her rocker."

Vicki inhaled sharply. "Georgia!"

"It's true, she's totally in love. But a little too totally, if you know what I mean," Georgia said.

"I know what you mean, and you shouldn't be making fun of her challenges."

"I'm not making fun, I'm just saying. Anyway, can we have brunch on Sunday? Like the good old days?" Georgia shuffled a pile of papers as she talked, glanced over the text, then signed where Diane had stuck a yellow flag.

"Is this about your concern for Emma, or is there something up with you?" Vicki said. "As much as we love to see you, you're not one to pop in for the sake of saying hello."

"What? I'm not allowed to want to see you guys?"

Vicki didn't reply. She knew her too well.

"The shit is really hitting the fan around here, and I'm feeling a little beaten to my knees over it." Georgia imagined Vicki's tiny frame holding her head in her lap and running her fingers through her hair. That's how Vicki always soothed her when she was younger.

"I can always count on you to tell it like it is," Vicki said. "I'll have a nice, juicy ham on the dining room table for one o'clock. Please show up while it's still hot."

"Thanks. I'll be there with my bib on." Georgia's mouth watered. She survived on energy bars, smoothies, and takeout most of the time. Vicki's cooking was always a treat.

"And in the meantime, remember who you are and how far you've come in your thirty-three years. I'm sure you can handle whatever life is throwing at you now."

"Thanks, Vicki. Say hi to Tom."

She hung up feeling so much better. She thought of tackling at least some of the paperwork on her desk, but the afternoon was slipping away on her. She signed another five documents and brought the pile out to Diane.

"Almost quitting time! Text me with the important stuff, otherwise enjoy your weekend. Gotta run."

She was going to hound Matt until he helped her fix at least one problem this week.

* * *

Matt sat at his desk looking at the color-coded pie charts on his monitor and tossed a piece of piping hot pizza between his hands. For all he knew, some housekeeping staff person had come in, dropped the syringe in the trash bin, and threw it out not knowing what it contained. Except, Ken was the only one who ever cleaned the fridge.

Out of the corner of his eye, he saw a white lab coat being waved from the doorway.

"Is it safe to enter? I come in peace," said the voice behind the white flag. It was Georgia.

"Why are you showing up on my turf when you told me to stay off yours?" he asked.

"The smell of the pizza drew me over. Mind if I join you?" Georgia walked in, grabbed a piece of pizza, and sat down across from him before he could answer.

"Do you have a habit of just taking what you want?" he said.

"Oh, now that hurts, Matt. I don't steal. May I?" She gingerly held the slice on her palm under her chin with the best imitation of puppy dog eyes he'd ever seen. He couldn't help but let his face melt into a smile, which she took as a yes.

"How is Ms. Jenkins this evening?" he asked.

"Barely hanging on. That's why I'm here. You mentioned something earlier about calling in a favor that could possibly help her?"

"That's what I said, but I've changed my mind."

"What do you mean? She's going to die," Georgia said.

"People die every day in this hospital." He put down his pizza and leaned back to better read her facial expressions. She was still absolutely gorgeous, but he was noticing fatigue and stress lines between her eyes. "I don't get it. You just had a patient bleed to death, all over you from what I saw earlier. You know death intimately. Why is Ms. Jenkins so special to you?" The split-second lapse in eye contact told him he was onto something.

"Who owes you a favor and what do they have that can help Ms. Jenkins?" she said instead of answering.

"Avoiding my question is not going to earn any of my trust, which is pretty much nonexistent at the moment," he said as he closed the pizza box cover.

"I didn't steal your cells," she said. "I have no interest in watching your study fail. I think you're onto something groundbreaking, and I really want you to succeed and change how we help heart patients."

Could she be more beautiful sitting there, sideways on the chair with her legs hanging over the armrest, her hair in a ponytail, not a bit of makeup on? The green of her scrubs complemented her hazel brown eyes. And those lips. Those lips were all he could ever focus on every time she came around him. He had to get a grip on himself. He was drooling over the woman who, for all he knew, could be ending his career.

There had to be more to this. She was almost obsessed. "Why Ms. Jenkins?"

"I already told you. Because her daughter will be in foster care if she dies."

"Thousands of kids go to foster care every year, Georgia."

A shadow crossed her face—an indication of the vulnerability she'd shown before. He pushed on. "Listen, if I give you anything, I'm asking for something in return. I want a reason. Either you tell me what's up or I don't make the phone call to get the ball rolling."

Georgia stood and threw her crust on the box on the desk. "I don't do blackmail." She took two steps before Matt got around his desk and grabbed her arm. His grip slackened instantly at the wave of electricity from her warm, soft skin.

"Don't go. Please. Talk to me," he said.

She turned to face him, closing the gap between them. She spoke so softly he had to lean in closer to hear.

"I never knew my father. My mom, Gail, was everything to me. She worked night shifts as a waitress and taught me to read when I was three. By the time I was in elementary school, she was teaching me from her GED textbooks. I was her world and she was mine for twelve years." Georgia paused, her voice still barely above a whisper.

"Then she died suddenly of a massive cardiac arrest and I had no one. I went into foster care. I bounced around for a bit. I had a bad experience with a couple who thought discipline with a belt would save my soul and that cleaning the wounds on my thighs with vinegar was love. Then, I had the best family in the world. I was just too hurt and bitter to realize it. When I was sixteen, and full of myself, I emancipated. First, I couch surfed and then lived on the streets. I worked three and then four jobs to put myself through med school.

"I would have given everything for one more day with my mother. I don't want Shawna to ever have to feel the loss I've lived with for twenty-one years."

She kept her chin up and her gaze steely. The only betrayal of her emotions was her shallow breathing and a swallow at the end of her speech, and that was all it took for Matt to feel like an absolute jerk for pushing her. He was sure she would have preferred to walk naked through the halls of Our Lady of Grace than to tell him her deepest secrets, especially after he accused her of sabotaging his study. Her lips were inches from his and he couldn't keep his eyes off them. Right when he found the resolve to lean in, she turned and grabbed another piece of pizza, and dropped back into her seat.

"Okay buddy, your turn for truth or dare," she said. The intimate moment seemed to be over. "Who else have you pissed off in the last two weeks who would want to ruin your project? Any estranged ex-wives or disgruntled lab rats kicking around?"

Matt sighed and sat down across the desk. "There's no ex-wife." A flash of pain hit his gut, but this was no time for swapping stories about dead loved ones. "I've had the same staff this whole time, and as far as I know they're all happy working here."

"Even though your study isn't getting its funding on time?" she said. "I'm sure your staff likes to get a paycheck every once in a while. Any of them hurting for bucks?"

His pulse cranked up a notch or two. Just when he was ready to trust her again she dropped another bomb on him. He was sure he'd never told her about the funding issues he was having. He hadn't told the hospital board either, so there was no way she could know that. How much more about his study did she know?

"I make sure my staff gets paid," he said.

"I'm assuming you're a smart enough man to have searched the rest of the lab in case the stuff was misplaced? Like the ketchup bottle hiding behind the milk?"

"Uh, yeah." Shit.

"Um, no. You didn't. It's written all over your face," she said. "Come on. Let's go have a look. I'll bet it was sitting there the whole time you were calling me a thief."

He hesitated, not knowing if he could completely trust her.

"Oh, come on, you wuss. If I'd stolen those cells, I wouldn't still be bugging you to help Ms. Jenkins."

"Maybe it's all a cover." The words came out a little too fast, and he quickly regretted them.

"Okay, now you're pissing me off," she said, standing. "I've got more important things to do than to sit here and be insulted. I'm going home. I gave you what you asked for and now you make the call—that was the deal. Text me when you reach that friend of yours and he gives me something concrete to work with."

She walked out. He didn't blame her. He was an ass. Matt couldn't take any more of the spreadsheets covering his two computer screens. He threw the now-empty pizza box in the garbage and locked up his office for the night.

He needed to clear his head of lusty thoughts and cloak-

and-dagger suspicions, so he headed for the pig's holding area.

"Mildred, it's your lucky day. I'm taking you for some fresh air before I go home."

He grabbed the pig's leash and they headed out the back to the service elevator. But only after double-checking the fridge to be sure he hadn't misplaced the stem cell syringe. Nope. Someone purposefully stole it.

Chapter 7

Emma shoved clothes into her closet and swept empty candy wrappers into a garbage pail, trying to reveal her bedroom under all the mess. She kicked some shoes under her bed, then crawled back under in search of the red stilettos—for Joe's enjoyment.

She hurried into the kitchen and started unpacking tonight's takeout. The place was a complete disaster. She abandoned the takeout and grabbed a big green garbage bag and started collecting empty takeout cartons and rotten food from the counters. She opened the window above the sink for a bit of fresh air.

What the hell was going on with her life? She was never this messy and disorganized as an adult. It seemed all she could think about lately was Joe and to hell with everything else. It took all she had to show up to work in a professional manner and perform her duties. The rest of her life was spent either with Joe or keeping herself busily distracted wanting to be with him. Could she spend the rest of her life with him? That thought stopped her in her tracks. No need to think about that now.

With a quick glance, she determined the kitchen was somewhat habitable and, with a cleared bed to screw on, the last things Emma needed were fewer clothes and a splash of perfume, which she sprayed in time for the doorbell to ring.

"Come in, baby," she called out.

"Hey, sexy—whoa," he said once inside. "Dinner and candles, and look at you. And those shoes." He took her into his arms and gave a rough half-kiss and half-bite down her neck. Electricity shot straight down her spine, sending heat of anticipation between her thighs. "We're going to have to eat fast. I won't be able to contain myself for too long."

"Anything to make my man happy. How was your day at work?" Her voice thickened with desire.

"I don't know. Dr. L. let me operate on my own, and I think I impressed her enough to get the job, but I didn't see her when I left. I came straight from assisting another surgery."

He leaned in for a deep kiss. His tongue licked her bottom lip and Emma knew this was the best drug-free high. Pure and utter bliss.

He pulled away and moved to her kitchen to pour two glasses of red wine. She raised her glass and delivered the news she knew would be the cherry on top of his wonderful day. "You know, Dr. L.—I mean Georgia—happens to be my best friend. We grew up in the same foster home. I was keeping it a secret until now. I'm sweet-talking you into her good books."

"Are you kidding me? That is a total game changer! Oh, Emma, I do love you." He gave her a full-body hug.

"Let's get some food into you so you can show me how much you love me, over and over, all weekend," she said.

Joe grabbed a chicken leg off the table, bit off a chunk of meat, and pulled her into the bedroom. "I'm hungrier for you," he said as he chewed.

Within seconds he had the hooks of her corset undone and his lips on her nipples. She fumbled with his buttons, too drunk with desire to make her hands work. He took over and stripped down. He turned her around, bent her over the bed and bit her tenderly on the ass. She squealed in delight. He pushed her onto her tummy and licked and kissed down the back of her legs, stopping to tickle the back of her knees with his teeth, then moved on to kiss her ankles. Every sensation made her moan with unbelievable need. Then he flipped her over, knelt in front of her, and raised her legs to his shoulders.

"These shoes are so fucking hot," he growled. He slipped her panties off, dragging them up her legs and over her shoes.

Then his cell phone rang. The shrill sending her crashing to reality with the sharpness of breaking glass.

"No, no, no. Don't answer it, Joe. Please," she begged.

"I have to. It's from Dr. L."

"You're off all weekend," she pleaded. "I've been waiting for this all day. Don't call her back." But it was a useless command as he already had the cell phone to his ear, his erection beckoning her.

"What's up? Now? I'm sort of in the middle of something… She died? I don't know… Okay, I'll be right over." Joe stood up and started to get dressed.

"No! You can't leave." Her heart sank at the reality that their evening was getting cut short.

"I won't be long my sweet, juicy love bug. I'm just running in to settle something quick. Besides, look at this rock-hard erection. You know I'm coming back to get this taken care of, right?"

He kissed her quickly, then was gone.

"I'll take care of that erection with a little bondage to keep you from running back to work again," she whispered.

Emma rolled to her bedside table and took out her vibrator. She'd used the gag gift a whole lot more since she'd started dating Joe. Her growing hunger had to be fed.

* * *

Georgia knocked on the X-ray box inside the morgue's entrance and called out a hello as she made her way into the autopsy room. Every morgue smelled and looked the same to her. Ceramic tile and metal tables leading to drains, sinks, and scales, and X-ray machines on every wall, enough tools to build a doghouse, and the same scent—throat-grabbing formaldehyde laced with stomach contents and blood. Dr. Jill David was hard at work on a young man riddled with bullets.

"Well, hello there Dr. Laurence. To what do I owe the visit?" she said.

"You've got a patient of mine on your to-do list, Nancy Reynolds. Any way we can speed her case up?" Georgia learned early on, as a teen surviving on her own, that the quickest way to results was to ask for what she wanted. She could get over hearing someone say no. Not asking meant waiting and not having any control.

"You've got to be kidding me," Jill said. "After this drive-by victim here, I have a bunch of stupid teens who either OD'd or had a suicide pact. Besides, it's the weekend when all the drunk and disorderly crimes start trickling in. What do you need an autopsy for?"

"Apparently I fucked up and the family wants my head on a platter," Georgia said, picking up a metal retractor and twisting the gear to close it. "Dr. Douglas won't let me in the OR until you're done."

"Wow. You must have really screwed up," Jill said. "Well, we don't want you hanging around here giving anybody the idea that you're swaying my findings. Go home and enjoy your time off for a change." What was her reputation that the pathologist knew she needed a weekend off?

"Yeah, yeah. First I have a resident's ass to chew." Georgia waved thanks on her way out.

She headed back to her office in time to meet Joe turning the corridor. She had maybe five strides to decide if she should be disciplining him or herself for the mess they both created with Nancy Reynolds.

"Hey there, lover boy. How's Emma doing?"

"Ah, yes, it turns out you know her, hey? She's great," he said. "We were having, uh, dinner when you called though, so if we can get this over with soon, it will make her much happier." They walked into her office and Georgia motioned him to sit down, implying he was not going back to Emma any time soon.

"Yeah, dinner, right," she said. "What you missed while you were rubbing elbows with Dr. Williams in the OR this afternoon was that Mrs. Reynolds bled to death all over the surgical intensive care unit. Apparently, that nick you felt, in combination with blood thinners, is not conducive to life."

"But it was just a needle poke," he said. "And you said yourself that you didn't see it."

"Yeah, well, when I opened her up it was more than a nick, it was a large bore puncture." She watched Joe's face for some indication that he knew what she was talking about, but she saw nothing.

"I don't know how you could have missed that, Dr. L."

"Neither do I. Tell me one more time what happened." She stared at the ceiling stretching shoulders that were rock-hard with tension.

"I was closing up and getting ready to suture the pericardium and I felt a little drag on my needle then suddenly the heart rate dropped, and everyone was in panic stations. I assumed that I had grazed the heart with my suture needle."

"Okay," she said. A needle drag would never cause what killed Mrs. Reynolds. It had to be something post-op. Could it be a nursing error? Was that fucking Marion her nurse post-op? She made a mental note to follow-up with Tracey.

"Okay? That's it?" He stood, apparently ready to bolt. Georgia pointed to the chair for him to sit back down.

"Not unless you have any other bright ideas to curing Ms. Jenkins."

"I gave you all I've got. Dr. Mancini's not pushing ahead on the human trials?"

"He's hit a few bumps in the road. But he's looking into something else for me." Her head started to ache from the weight of the day. Possibly also from dehydration. She couldn't remember the last thing she drank.

"What else does he think he's going to find? He's not a heart surgeon. He has what we need—those stem cells. He's seen what Ms. Jenkins is up against right now." Joe's frustration hitched his voice.

"Don't you worry your pretty little head," she said. She pointed to the door. "Now, go write up an incident report about your needle dragging on the ventricle during closing and the deceleration that followed. And make sure a copy gets sent to the morgue for the autopsy. Then run along home to Emma. And make sure she can still walk on Sunday. We have brunch—"

"Whoa, an incident report?" Joe said, suddenly not just antsy, but angry. "That goes on my record. I can't have that on my file." Joe's about-face almost made her dizzy.

"No, it goes on mine," she said. "I was responsible. The beauty of a teaching hospital means my ass is on the line. No OR privileges for me until after the autopsy."

"Even more reason to just let this blow over, Dr. L. What good will a recommendation be from you if you've lost your license to practice?" he said. For a split second, she'd thought it was her career he was concerned about. Or at least the patient's life. Having only one attending position open was making all the residents even more self-absorbed than the surgeon ego required.

"Listen, write the report and go home. I've got it all under control. All of it. Your career, mine, and Ms. Jenkins. It's all going to work out."

She internally repeated her surgical preceptor's most

profound mantra—"fake it 'til you make it"—as she walked Joe out.

* * *

Georgia grabbed a vitamin water from her mini-fridge and changed into her jogging gear before locking her office. If she'd ever needed a run before, she definitely needed one now. Her head buzzed with one problem after the other.

In the elevator, she worried about Ms. Jenkins. Her options were very few at this point and she was keeping the big guns to the very last minute because most of what she had left to offer Ms. Jenkins would only last seventy-two hours, and she didn't like the odds of playing against a ticking clock. Time usually won.

The brisk evening air hitting Georgia's face both bit and soothed her. This was her heaven. One step in front of the other, she headed to the lake. Her heart rate climbed as she pushed herself harder, knowing sweat would soon be trickling down her back.

But thoughts rushed in again. She worried about Shawna holding her own, all alone, with a drug-addicted aunt as a custodian. She knew social services couldn't be held at bay forever, and even if she miraculously got a heart for Ms. Jenkins tonight, recovery would be a long road. She wondered wildly if social services would let her take Shawna in.

What are you thinking, woman?

The whole reason she had no romantic life was specifically to avoid the responsibility of a family. Why would she voluntarily take in a girl at the most vulnerable time of her life when she was grieving the loss of a mother? Sometimes she could hardly take care of herself. She told herself the chances were slim that anyone would award her custody with all the damned conflict of interest shit they'd throw at her, plus her long work hours and now being under the microscope at work. Those lost and scared brown eyes came into view in her mind's eye and she realized she'd ask about fostering Shawna on Monday anyway.

And what the hell was going on with Emma and Joe? He was the best chief resident, always had been, and he was her favorite. He should know that by now. It was like Joe and Emma were so love-drunk they'd lost touch with reality. She would talk to Emma at Tom and Vicki's brunch on Sunday and ease Emma's mind a little about Joe's career options. She would also try to get Emma to take her medication again. Her ADHD could very well account for her obsessing over Joe.

Georgia's lungs burned from the rush of forced breath, yet she was thankful for the fresh spring-like air. She raced past a man walking his dog and a mom pushing a stroller. Both looked mortified at her drenched and flushed state. She pushed on.

The last overwhelming stressor in her life that she couldn't ignore anymore was dealing with Matt Mancini. She'd never met a man who, despite his accusing her of a crime, she desperately wanted to hold.

He almost made a puddle out of her when he pushed her on why she cared so much about Ms. Jenkins. He'd asked her for the most vulnerable thing she could ever give up to anyone—the truth about her past. And he'd topped that by accusing her of making it all up to cover for stealing the cells. That had to be grounds for murder somewhere in the world. Yet, all she could think about was those strong sexy hands holding her tight. Maybe there was something in the water making everybody love-drunk.

She looped around and sprinted back toward the hospital, trying to clear the last image of Matt holding her naked body out of her mind.

* * *

"What a day, Mildred! Are you as tuckered out as I am?" Matt rubbed his stomach, not knowing if the heartburn was from the pizza or talking to Georgia. Either way, he was glad to be settling Mildred into her pen and heading home. Researchers didn't usually lead this kind of stressful existence. He took the back stairs and stepped out the same door he'd taken Mildred out of for her walk and toward the parking lot. His black BMW, with personalized CELL MD plates, was his second love after his bike. Though it was considered a luxury car, it wasn't anything compared to the cars Phil owned.

He'd purposefully parked farther from the lamppost. He liked to leave the added safety of parking under the bright lights for women. When the car was in gear and he tried to back out, the flopping of rubber alerted Matt to a major problem. He got out of the car.

All four of his tires were slashed.

"Oh, come on." Who the hell does this to a BMW? He looked around at the other cars. None of them were vandalized. He went back into the car, nothing was missing. He had a leather bag and a spare designer suit in the back seat, both would have been worth some resale money if whoever did this broke into the car. This was obviously a targeted act of vandalism.

He scanned the perimeter of the parking lot. In the distance, he saw a yellow windbreaker bouncing beyond the trees. He hit the remote locks and ran after the person. It didn't take him long to catch up, as the jogger was slowing as they approached him. It was none other than Georgia Laurence.

Suspect number one.

Again.

"Hey, what are you doing? Hey!" he shouted at her.

"Hey to you too." She walked in place and panted while fiddling with the Garmin strapped to her arm.

"What are you running from?" he asked.

"The Boogeyman." She paused for a few deep breaths. "I'm not running from anything, you dingbat. It's called exercise. You should try it. I've heard there are many health benefits associated with it." She continued to catch her breath between words.

"How long you been at it?"

"About seventeen years now, I guess," she said, grinning.

"No, I mean tonight," he said. His patience with her smartass remarks was wearing quite thin.

"Why are you asking? More cells go missing and I'm taking the fall for those too?" She turned her Garmin to him while she spoke. An hour and twenty-two minutes, ten miles. What did he think that was going to prove? He had no idea when his tires were slashed.

"No, I put a lock on the fridge. My tires were slashed when I got to my car a few minutes ago."

Her face paled. "Really? You sure you haven't pissed anybody off lately?"

"Just you," he said. He crossed his arms over his chest.

"Yeah, you're getting really good at that, but that's because you're not clueing in to get to know me better. First, I'd never steal, and second, if you pissed me off enough, I'd cause bodily harm. I wouldn't waste my time on your tires."

Georgia's phone rang.

"Oh, shit! Code blue on Ms. Jenkins."

They ran together to the hospital entrance.

Chapter 8

"Somebody page Dr. Carter and get him in here, stat!" Georgia yelled as soon as she walked into the room. Brian, the first-year resident, was running the code. He was red-faced as only a fair-skinned redhead could get. They made quite the pair with her fresh-from-a-run appearance.

"I've got it from here, Brian. You stand back and take notes. Who's the nurse in charge of Ms. Jenkins?"

The nurse doing the compressions, Chloe, one of Georgia's favorites, spoke up. "Me."

"Brian, do the compressions so I can talk to Chloe." The resident appeared relieved to have some part in the code, but not one where he'd have to think of anything.

"What are her latest 'lytes and oxygen levels?" Georgia asked.

"Her creatinine was 1.1 and her potassium was 3.4, her CO_2 was forty-one and her O_2 was ninety-two."

"Okay, that's not it. What do you think it is, Chloe?"

"Her output has been dwindling all day, as you know," Chloe said. "I think it hit its lower limit."

"Let's put a balloon in her then. Somebody get me the stuff to do an arterial groin line. Someone else, get the machine."

Matt caught her eye at the side of the room. "Everybody, this is Dr. Matt Mancini from the research department. Matt, this is everybody." The usual cast of code attendants were all present. They all said "hi" while they rushed around the room.

"Matt, this is my last resort. I can't leave this balloon in forever. The risk of infection and perforation of the aorta are too high. I need that expert you were calling for me. Ms. Jenkins and Shawna need a miracle."

Her pleading was interrupted by Joe showing up, face flushed with his hair all tousled. At least he had clothes on.

"What happened?" he asked.

"Her heart is tired. It's giving up," Georgia said. "I'm putting in an intra-aortic balloon pump. Go wash your hands and get us some sterile gowns."

Matt called out from the door to the room, "I'm going to make that call now, Georgia. I'll be right back."

She gave him the best smile she could muster at the moment and mouthed a thank you.

Equipment started filling the ICU room. Joe returned looking more presentable and commanded the team with orders to get the balloon pump into Ms. Jenkins. Georgia admired his speed and skill. Within minutes Ms. Jenkins had a heartbeat and her oxygen levels were coming up.

* * *

Matt unlocked his office door and flicked on the lights. The scene was one straight out of a Law and Order episode. The chairs were toppled and his filing cabinets were all open, papers strewn everywhere. He was starting to think that Georgia was right. Someone was quite pissed at him. He had a closer look to see what was missing and his overhead bookshelf had a hole where the procedure manual for the stem cell trial should have been. He ran to the locked refrigerator to check if the remaining cells were still there.

The fridge was still locked and, when he opened it, he found the last three syringes all accounted for. Did that mean the perpetrator was still holding on to the last batch and needed the protocol to use it? Maybe he needed to start to think about someone outside of the hospital, maybe some terrorists from another country?

Don't be ridiculous, Matt. You can't kill someone with stem cells! This isn't chemical warfare.

No, he was right to think of someone in the hospital, and if it wasn't Georgia trying to cure Ms. Jenkins at any cost, then maybe it was some zealot trying to stop the progress of stem cell research itself.

Either way, he had to get to the bottom of it without losing the study. That's what they'd want after all, for his study to fail. He returned to his office and quickly tidied up while he dialed Dr. Childs' home number.

"Bruce. It's Matt Mancini."

"It's the weekend, Matt. What the hell do you want?" The frigid reception didn't shock him.

"It's payback time." He leaned back in his chair and ran a hand over his exhausted face, trying to stimulate some feeling back into it.

"What are you talking about?" Bruce asked.

"You know that paper you got co-author credits on that you actually did no work on? I'm calling to have the favor returned." He still hated himself for going against his better judgment and personal ethics by giving Bruce credit on that paper. He just hoped the karma of the returned favor balanced things out.

"You want your name on a new cardiac medication paper?"

"No, I want you and your new medication to pay a little visit to Albany. We have a patient that needs your expertise yesterday."

"I'm supposed to play in a golf tournament this weekend." Of course you were, Matt thought. Thank God he never caught the golfing bug.

"Cancel it."

Silence hung, then: "After this, I don't owe you jack."

"Yup, after this we can forget we ever met."

"I'll book a flight and be there by noon tomorrow."

"Good." The line went dead.

Matt finished cleaning, making sure nothing else had been taken. Then he had a good look at his office door lock. No sign of forced entry as far as a mere research doctor could tell. There were so many master keys in a hospital, anybody with enough determination could find their way into any room.

He did his best thinking while brainstorming with another person. He needed someone he could trust to bounce his ideas off of, and he already assigned Ken the early morning wake-up. Georgia was the only other person he could talk to about this. But could he trust her?

Had she had enough time to come in here and do this to his office, slash his tires, and go for a jog? It didn't add up or seem likely. He saw earnest vulnerability on her face when she stood in his office and bared her soul.

He could argue that he called in the favor from Dr. Childs for the sake of Ms. Jenkins, but he'd be lying to himself if he didn't admit to also hoping to impress Georgia. He couldn't deny the pull she had on him. What he had to figure out was if that attraction was clouding his better judgment, causing him to trust her with the one thing he could one-up his brother with. Oh, to watch Phil squirm as he received the Nobel Prize in Medicine.

He headed back to intensive care. For all he knew there was no Ms. Jenkins left to save.

* * *

Georgia observed the waves of blood pressure and cardiac output undulate on the monitor, pleased with the whole team's effort at stabilizing Ms. Jenkins once again.

"Thanks, everyone. I guess I'll go find an on-call room to settle into for the night."

"No way, I'm staying Dr. L.," Joe said. "This is your weekend off. Brian and I can handle the rest of the night. Besides, she's stable now."

"You sure Emma won't have us both killed for this?" she joked.

"It's my job. She knows that. And I'll have fun making it up to her later."

"Oh, gross," Georgia said. "That's the closest thing I have to a sister you're feeling up."

"Sorry," he said, grinning.

"Call me on my cell at the slightest change."

She walked over to the computer and finished off her charting. A hand tenderly touched her shoulder.

"Can I have a word with you, in private?" Matt leaned in and spoke softly in her ear, sending a thrill up her spine.

"Sure. I'm about to sign off. Want to walk me to my Uber? No way I'm walking home tonight." she asked, willing her heart to relax.

"Yeah, I'd offer you a ride home, but it looks like I'll be hitting up a ride tonight myself."

Georgia finished typing and signed herself out of the terminal, then led the way to the elevator. They stood enveloped in a heavy silence as they waited for the elevator car to arrive. He avoided her gaze. His forehead was etched with stress lines and his shoulders slumped as if he carried the weight of the world on his back.

Once they were in the elevator, Georgia turned to him. "This feels like a good news, bad news kind of announcement. So, hit me with the good stuff first."

"Dr. Bruce Childs is flying in tomorrow morning to enroll Ms. Jenkins in his study."

"The Bruce Childs. Oh my God. How did you do that?" she said. This could be everything she'd wished for. "I've been bugging him for years to partner with our hospital on trials. Oh, Matt, thank you, thank you, thank you!"

She threw herself into his arms and planted a kiss right on his lips. He held her close to him a few seconds more than she'd intended to stay. Her mind told her to back away from him—professionalism and all that bullshit—but her body was quite happy right there in his arms. She leaned in, searching for another slower, softer kiss, but the doors opened and the lobby lights destroyed their solitude. They both let go and walked out into a lobby that was empty save for a security guard at his post dutifully solving a crossword puzzle.

"That takes care of the good news. What's the bad news?" she asked.

"I can't say here."

"Shall we share a cab then and we'll talk in the car until you drop me off?" Her body hummed at the thought of spending more time near his.

Chapter 9

They hopped into the Uber and Matt started recounting how he found his office and what was missing.

"Holy shit." She matched his hushed tone.

"I'm going to have to broaden my list of suspects. I'm starting to think that maybe a religious group intends to sabotage the study, even though we use skin cells, not embryonic cells. Who do you know on the board or on staff that would—"

The car had stopped. The driver turned and announced the first address they'd given him.

"We're at my place already," Georgia said. "Come in and we'll figure this out."

Matt paid the driver while Georgia shot her doorman a death stare for his surprise at her bringing home a man.

At her door, she announced, "I have a dog. I have to run him outside for a minute."

"I love dogs," Matt said, smiling. You remember the family dog when you dated Phil? Our springer spaniel, Bentley, who loved to hump your leg every time you walked through the door? He never did that with anyone else but you, come to think of it."

"Oh my God, I was so mortified." She laughed out loud. His smile could melt ice. She wanted another kiss so bad. She forced herself to focus on the task at hand. He was being targeted by some madman.

They opened the door and Gus leaped off the couch, wagging his tail harder than she'd ever seen before. He sat in front of Matt and offered his paw without being asked. She hoped Matt's focus on Gus made up for the lack of Better Homes decor in her apartment.

"Wow, Gus, you're one amazing suck-up." She grabbed his leash and snapped it on his collar. "Grab a bottle of wine from the rack and pour us each a glass, will you? I'll be right back."

Gus probably wanted to be back in Matt's company as much as she did, because he did his business in record time. Before long, all three of them were sitting on her couch. Soft music, wine, and an overweight hound between Georgia and Matt. It was almost romantic.

"Okay, so we've got stolen cells, then slashed tires and a stolen procedure book," Georgia said, ticking off each criminal act on her fingers. "Why would they slash your tires? You would automatically go back to your office to call someone about them. Did they want you to see the mess?"

"Maybe they is right," Matt said. "Maybe one person trashed my office while another slashed my tires. They had to be following me to know I wasn't at either location."

"Tell me again why we're not calling the cops on this?" Georgia asked, then sipped her wine. She'd spent a good amount of her youth avoiding authority of all kinds. She knew lots of people who avoided the cops for various reasons, but she tended to stay clear of anything illegal herself and Matt didn't seem like the type to snub authority.

"Because I can't take the chance that the oversight committee will shut down the trial. There are so many layers of checks and balances for ethics and procedure. My every move and decision are evaluated for the soundness of the research," he said.

"But missing cells have nothing to do with the trial results being flawed or the trial being unethical," she said.

"No, but California is already a pain in the neck," he said. "We're supposed to be a team working together, reproducing each other's results. But they want their names first on the publication. They want the glory so bad that they're doing everything to make my part in the study look like an afterthought. I don't want them to have any excuse to cut me out of the study and hoard all the prestige."

"Could they be the ones screwing things up for you?" Georgia asked.

"I don't know. I'd like to think they have the same drive to help humanity that we do. Besides, I doubt a stranger from California could be lurking around the hospital unnoticed all this time." Matt seemed to consider for a moment more. "Unless they paid someone off? Someone from Our Lady of Grace?"

They sat in silence and enjoyed the fourth movement of Bizet's L'Arlésienne Suite No. 2. Georgia topped off their wine, and the movement on the couch finally shooed the dog to his second-favorite spot on the loveseat. Georgia's phone lit up with a text. It was from Emma. Some long ramble about Joe and sex and a bunch of curse words. Emma must have used voice to text because half of it didn't make sense. It wasn't about Ms. Jenkins so Georgia would get back to that later.

"Your turn for truth or dare, Doctor. Why's this study so important to you? There are millions of studies out there. Why's it so important you don't lose this one to the Californians?" Georgia cocked her head to the side.

"You mean besides saving lives and having spent the last seven years of my career on it?" he said.

"Yeah."

"My brother is an asshole," he said.

"I know. I dated him, remember?" For as short as their relationship had been, the Mancini family became her second family. She understood their family dynamics intimately.

"He could have told our family that I tried to keep him from taking the sailboat out alone, but he didn't. He milked their sympathy for him all this time at my expense," he said, the passion of it immediately flushing his cheeks. "He even had to go into ortho, like Dad. I really want to rub something in his face for a change. And this is the kind of study that's going to make international headlines. This will win me awards."

His face was riddled with anger and openness and sorrow. Georgia longed for his smile again, the one that crinkled the sides of his eyes. She did the only thing she could think of—the one thing that could bring happiness back to the moment. She leaned in for a kiss.

Their lips stayed locked when they put the wine glasses on her makeshift coffee table and as they stood. The kiss turned from consolation and tenderness to raw desire and passion. Georgia led Matt to her bedroom, closing the door behind them before Gus had a chance to follow.

As Georgia started to unbutton Matt's shirt, she realized she was still wearing her running gear, which also meant she was covered in the powdery film of dried, salty sweat. There was no way she was letting him anywhere near her nether regions after a run, which only left one option. She gently placed her finger on his lips and led him to her en suite bathroom.

She felt Matt's eyes on her every move as she stepped out of her Lulus and into the shower, gesturing for him to join her under the warm water. He dropped his pants dropped instantly, baring a generous erection. Their mouths found each other again as their hands wandered over every inch of slick skin. Georgia's breath caught in her throat as Matt gently caressed her nipples with soapy fingers.

He continued to explore her beneath the foam and washed her entire body, spending extra time on her clitoris as he rinsed off the bubbles and replaced the water with his skillful tongue. Once she moaned her release, he lifted her onto his erection and brought them both to their first climax of the evening.

* * *

After a night full of lovemaking, they woke in each other's arms partially covered with a bedsheet. Georgia couldn't believe how gorgeous the man lying next to her was and how artful a lover he was. She turned to her bedside clock. Seven. Her cell hadn't rung. They both probably needed another five hours' sleep, but she needed to check on Ms. Jenkins herself and he needed to arrange a vehicle to pick up Dr. Childs at the airport.

"I'm heading to the shower again, Prince Charming. We've got to get a move on things."

"Umm... what time is it?" Matt asked, blinking the sleep out of his eyes.

"Seven."

"Okay, I'll meet you in there so we can kill two birds with one stone."

"What are you talking about?" she said.

"A good morning quickie while we wash up."

"You're insatiable!" she shouted.

She brushed her teeth while the shower warmed up and steam filled the bathroom. He approached her from behind and started massaging her breasts, then lead her into the shower. She luxuriated in the wet ripples of water that rolled down her skin beneath his hands.

Having enjoyed themselves for a little too long, they rushed out of the washroom and dressed. They walked to work together and grabbed breakfast from Starbucks on the way. A mere six hours after they had left the night before, they were back in the hospital lobby. No further ahead in solving either of their puzzles, but in a much better state of relaxation.

"Thank you for a wonderful evening, Dr. Mancini," Georgia said.

"And for a spectacular morning, Dr. Laurence. I'll call your cell as soon as I have Dr. Childs with me. First, I'd better go call the garage and get some new tires on my car."

* * *

Georgia headed for the surgical intensive care unit before going to her office. She had to check on Ms. Jenkins herself. She walked into the dimly lit corridor flanked by equipment carts and banks of glass sliding doors. The nursing station was a hub of activity as the night nurses updated the day shift.

"We were about to page you, Dr. Laurence," Donna said as she approached the nurses' station.

"What's going on?"

"Everything is fine, Ms. Jenkins is stable. It's just that Shawna is here and asking questions about the new equipment." She said pointing over her shoulder.

"Joe never called last night, how did it all go?" Georgia asked.

"Like a well-oiled machine. There's Dr. Carter now." He was approaching the nurses' station.

"Hey, Joe," Georgia said. "I can take it from here. You go crawl into bed at home."

"Thanks, Dr. L.," he said. "A good breakfast and a few more hours' sleep and I'll be good to take the night shift again tonight. I hit the books last night looking for anything we can do differently—"

Georgia interrupted him. "I'll fill you in after your nap, but we've got a very important surprise flying in this morning."

"A heart?" he said, looking hopeful.

"You're the one who's been here all night, don't you think you'd have heard about a heart before I would, shit for brains?" she said affectionately. "No, something to tide us over. Go get some more sleep so you start making sense again, boy." They both smiled and she faked punching his arm. "And I said sleep, not the horizontal tango with Emma."

"No promises there, boss."

Georgia's cell rang. It was Matt. She walked out of the nurses' station to take the call.

"Miss me already?" she breathed.

"Ken didn't come in for work this morning and he's not answering his cell or home phone."

Chapter 10

Just when Georgia thought she was going to have a smooth day. "I assume this is out of character for Ken?" she asked.

"Very. I have four hours to find him and get my car fixed and pick up Dr. Childs."

She called out to Joe. "Wait a second, Joe."

"Meet me in the parking lot," Georgia said into her phone. "I'll have a car for us in two minutes. We'll go to Ken's apartment."

"Joe, you drive a car to work, don't you?" she said.

"Yes," he said cautiously. "And I drive it back home too."

"Okay, you want to impress your boss for that attending position?" she said. "Stay a couple more hours and give me the keys to your car."

"Anything your heart desires, my lady." He dug his car keys out of his front jeans pocket and handed them over. "It's the red Honda in the east parking lot. Plate says HART CUTR."

"Yuck, that's gory." Georgia crinkled her nose.

"I couldn't fit cardiac surgeon on a plate," he said with a shrug.

Donna, still sitting at the nurses' station, raised an eyebrow at Georgia, then looked toward Ms. Jenkins' room.

She needed to meet Matt, but Shawna had her full attention for the next few minutes. She made her way into Ms. Jenkins' room, sat beside Shawna, and took her hand.

"I only have a few seconds, sweetie," Georgia said. "But though this machine is a last resort, doing the work for your mom's heart, I want you to know we're flying in a research doctor from Baltimore who will do whatever he can to help us out. The nurses can answer any of your questions in the meantime, okay?"

"Thanks, see you later Dr. Laurence." Shawna's face softened with hope.

* * *

Georgia met up with a very frazzled Matt in the back stairwell. Something was drastically wrong.

"This is about more than a missing researcher," she said.

"The lock was broken on the fridge and another batch of cells is gone."

"Shit! Do you think it's Ken?" They took the stairs down to the parking lot.

"I would never have guessed it," he said. "I trust him completely. I need to find him. I need to know the truth. At least now I'm sure it wasn't you because we were together last night."

Her breath caught in her throat for a split second. She spotted Joe's car and led them to it. "Here's the car, and the keys. You drive since you know where we're going."

Georgia sat in the car in silence. How could he say that she was only now in the clear of suspicion? Did he sleep with her last night while still not trusting her completely? Was that all she was, a romp in the sack? He took the opportunity that was presented to him even if he didn't remotely trust her?

She felt dirty to be in the same car as him now. It took everything in her to not string every insult she could think of at him. She'd tolerate him until Dr. Childs was in her office then he'd never see her face again. How could she have fallen for another Mancini brother?

"You're awfully quiet over there," he said.

"I'm thinking." Did that come out as curt as she meant it?

Her cell phone rang. "Dr. Laurence here."

"Where the hell is my boyfriend? It's his weekend off you know." Emma's voice dripped with fury.

"Emma, it's really not a good day to get on my last frayed nerve. By the way, I got your message last night. Thanks for the poetic name-calling there, sis."

"I didn't send you any messages last night," Emma said.

"What the hell is going on, Emma?" Georgia meant that as a figure of speech because her patience ran way too thin to get into what was really going on.

"Listen, I want Joe to have the rest of the weekend off or I'll contact the head of the hospital and tell him you're abusing your residents."

Oh, yeah. Dr. Douglas was another thorn in her side she'd conveniently forgotten about.

"He'll be home in about an hour," she spat back. "You do realize we have some very sick people to tend to, right? Cut us all a little slack, little Miss Nine to Five, Monday to Friday sitting behind a desk. Lay off my case."

She hung up, hating the anti-climactic swiping of an icon instead of slamming a receiver into the cradle.

"We're here," Matt said.

They rang the apartment buzzer and no one answered. Finally, a tiny elderly woman with her arms full of Yorkshire terriers needed a hand with the front door, which allowed them entrance into the building. They ran up four flights of stairs to Ken's apartment.

Matt was about to knock when they saw the door was already open. They called out to Ken, but there was no answer. As they turned the corner to the living room, they found Ken laying in a pool of blood. There was a butcher knife sticking out of his chest and a note beside it, moist with blood. Georgia knelt to feel for a carotid pulse while Matt read the note out loud.

Don't try to stop me or Georgia is next.

Matt turned to lean on the wall, obviously not used to so much blood and death. The fact that it was his friend, a man he shared his professional life with every day, lying dead at their feet probably didn't help. Georgia forced herself to stay clinical. She'll deal with the death threat in a minute, for now, they needed to call the cops.

She took out her cell and started to dial 911.

"What are you doing?" Matt reached out and took her phone.

"Calling the cops," she said.

"We can't get the police involved!" he said. "That'll stop the research dead in its tracks."

"There's a dead guy at your feet," she said, frustrated with his singlemindedness. "We have to report it!"

"But the note clearly links this to my study."

"It's only clear to you," she said. "Stick it in your pocket and we'll say he didn't show up for work." Georgia grabbed her phone back.

"You mean you'll keep the fact that someone threatened to kill you quiet, for me?"

She thought long and hard about her options, about how much she hated Matt at the moment, about how vulnerable he was last night when he told her how important this trial was to him. Then she thought of the one goal she'd had all along.

"No, not for you. For Ms. Jenkins. I want you to use her for your first human trial by Wednesday. That gives you four days to fix up your numbers or practice on more pigs out on a farm or something, but I am not sticking my neck out for you without something in return." She touched the last number one in 911, disgusted with their lack of ethics. All those years surviving on her own, she never broke the law. But whenever she looked into Shawna's face as she sat holding her mother's hand she remembered the pain she went through when she lost her own mother. She didn't kill Ken. She's saving Sandra's life. She's just withholding evidence and blackmailing the man she slept with a few hours ago. But she could live with that for now.

"911, what's your emergency?"

"Someone has been murdered."

Chapter 11

Officer Richards and Officer Hall seemed satisfied with Matt and Georgia's story. The cops left their cards in case they thought of any pertinent information later.

Georgia was glad to get away from the murder scene. She was used to the metallic odor of fresh blood, but it was usually in a well-ventilated, sterile environment. Ken's cramped and stuffy apartment made her feel like she was inside the corpse.

She couldn't read Matt's expression or body language. He seemed all over the map; nervous, scared, sad, angry, relieved, and quizzical. He put his hand on her shoulder when he opened the car door for her, a tender touch that nauseated her.

Her life was threatened, and her response was to blackmail Matt into breaking protocol and ethics and to hide a note from the law. What the hell was she thinking? And who the hell was doing all this shit?

The realization of the death threat started to sink in and Georgia suddenly got a chill she couldn't shake off. She wrapped her arms around herself. Why would someone want her dead? Why would someone want to ruin a breakthrough study at the cost of human lives? And at the cost of her own life.

She had nothing to do with this study. She only stumbled upon it two days ago. She was only implicated by being with Matt. Someone saw them together. But they weren't *together* together until last night in her apartment. Could they have been watched?

She turned to look at Matt. No matter how much she wanted to hate him right now, she didn't regret sleeping with him. It was a phenomenal few hours of her life. He was clearly in agony now.

"Listen, you're going to have to take a cab to pick up Dr. Childs," she said. "Joe needs his car."

"You still want me to get Dr. Childs?"

"Well, yes. Ms. Jenkins needs cardiac output right now and I'm not allowed in the operating room yet. We have to use what Dr. Childs has in the meantime."

"Fine. You win," he said.

He tossed the keys at her over the hood of the car and they went their separate ways.

* * *

Georgia headed straight to Ms. Jenkins' room. Shawna was there, and Georgia sat beside the bed and held Shawna's hand. She needed somebody, anybody. The closest thing she had to a family was royally pissed with her at the moment, her closest work colleague, who messed up so bad it might cost her job, was off to take care of her angry sister, hopefully. And the man she'd fallen so hard and fast for last night turned into a completely different person once the sun came up.

"What are they teaching you kids in school these days?" Georgia asked Shawna with a forced smile.

"Well, Mom wants me to concentrate on my sciences, but I really love my music classes and language arts."

"What's language arts?"

"A fancy name for English," Shawna said.

"I see." She rubbed Shawna's small hand in hers.

"Mom's okay, right?" said Shawna. "I mean, the nurses are all much happier with her today, but you seem a million miles away, and I hate to tell you, but you're not half as funny as usual."

"Sorry, I've got a bunch of other things on my mind

besides your mom. Actually, your mom is the one good thing I have going on right now," Georgia said.

"Anything you want to talk about?" Shawna asked. "I can be a good listener."

"Oh, Shawna, you're a sweetheart, but the last thing you need right now is to hear my sob stories while your mother fights for her life in an ICU bed."

A nurse stepped into the room. "Dr. Mancini and Dr. Childs are here for you, Dr. Laurence."

"Here comes your mom's miracle." Georgia smiled at Shawna and patted her hand as she left the room.

She found the two men bent over Ms. Jenkins' chart. "Hello, gentlemen. Very nice to meet you, Dr. Childs, I'm Georgia Laurence. You've avoided me like the plague for about four years now."

She extended her hand as if she hadn't just cut him down at the knees.

"So sorry about that, Dr. Laurence. I obviously didn't have my priorities in the right order, now did I?" Dr. Childs said, smirking.

"So what kind of magic potion did you bring along?"

"Have you heard of the HART study over at Berkley and Johns Hopkins? That's us," Dr. Childs said. "We're finishing up our human trials of a new intravenous drip that works ten times better than milrinone and vasopressin. Your patient is much sicker than any of our research subjects, but with any luck, she'll be off the balloon pump and ticking along until her heart transplant date comes around."

"Please, impress me." Georgia waved the way to Ms. Jenkins' room.

Matt excused himself, saying he had work piling up in his office and that he'd return later to check on things.

The day moved along quickly as medications were adjusted after the experimental medication was started and

Ms. Jenkins began to turn the corner. The balloon pump was out by supper time and she was off the ventilator and talking to Shawna by the end of the evening shift.

Donna sat down with the day nurse and received the day's report, including the binder for Dr. Childs' study protocols. Georgia could not contain her smile at Donna's delight upon seeing Ms. Jenkins doing so much better.

Dr. Childs had left with Matt after the successful extubation, promising to call first thing in the morning for an update.

Georgia couldn't wait for Joe to come in and see the difference too. She hadn't heard from him all day, nor from Emma for that matter. She assumed they had a nice reunion and all was good in La La Land again.

Nothing could have prepared Georgia for the look of pure fury on Joe's face when he saw Ms. Jenkins sitting up in bed, her cheeks looking the healthiest it had been since she arrived.

"What happened?" Joe demanded.

"This here is because of a drug trial with Dr. Brian Childs. Matt Mancini is a good old friend and pulled some strings for me. She looks great, doesn't she?"

"Yeah. Except, I thought that we'd be the ones to fix her, not some stupid research goon." He flipped through the binder scanning the protocols.

"We still have to do a transplant, Joe. I know the scalpel is mightier than the pill and all that crap, but the point is she's doing much better," Georgia said. She understood the surgeon's ego all too well, but she was getting confused over what was pissing him off so much. "If she stays this way all evening, why don't you go home and leave Brian to keep an eye on things? It's both of our weekends off after all."

"It's okay. I think I exhausted Emma. I'll stay here until Monday. I can use the practice and you need your time off."

"Have it your way. Goodnight."

She went over to Ms. Jenkins' bedside and tucked the blanket around Shawna, who was fast asleep in the lounge chair beside her with a chemistry textbook open on her lap. She exchanged a smile with Ms. Jenkins, who whispered "thank you." Georgia felt relief in her own broken heart for the first time in a long time. She'd have to try to communicate to Tom and Vicki just how much she finally appreciated everything they did for her, even after she walked out on them. All they ever wanted for her was what she's wanted for Shawna. She just couldn't see it then. She couldn't let love in when she was a hurting sixteen-year-old. One more glance at the sleeping beauty and she knew for sure that she could never be responsible for a child's happiness and welfare. She could never trust herself to do the marriage and kids thing. Give her a scalpel and a suture needle any day, but don't ask her to be in charge of the emotions that come with a child's breaking heart.

Chapter 12

Georgia woke from a fitful sleep with her face in the pillow Matt had used. His smell alone aroused her senses but then she remembered why she'd slept so poorly. She'd had a mix of nightmares featuring a killer wielding a syringe full of stem cells and erotic dreams about Matt Mancini. She called the hospital and everything was as she left it the night before. All was well.

She dressed in her jogging gear and dragged Gus out for a quick jog, then showered and dressed for brunch with the family. She thought she'd stop by Emma's place first to see if she could smooth some feathers before they headed over to Tom and Vicki's house. It was a ten-minute walk and the spring day was beautiful. Quite a change, as her rare weekends off almost always had rain.

She rang and knocked but Emma didn't answer, so she dug out her spare key.

The place was a pigsty. The kitchen was full of dirty dishes, empty bottles of wine, and old takeout cartons. The living room had oily popcorn bags, candy wrappers, and trashy magazines strewn all over. Georgia walked into the bedroom, which reeked of sex. The sheets were rumpled and the bedside table had a pile of condom wrappers on one side and sex toys on the other. Lacy lingerie hung on the lamps and treadmill.

"What the hell went on in this place last night?" she said to herself.

Actually, she didn't want to know. The evidence was more than she could handle. She'd known Emma most of her life and this was not her Emma. She'd clearly gone way over the edge with her ADHD. Or maybe there was something else at play.

Hopefully, Emma was at Tom and Vicki's right now because they all clearly needed to have a long talk.

* * *

Georgia pulled up to the old farmhouse at the end of the long lane. Vicki greeted Georgia with open arms before she even got to the door. Clearly, she'd watched her drive up from the kitchen window. Vicki looked great for a sixty-five-year-old grandmother of five. In addition to the two children Vicki and Tom officially adopted, Emma and Zach, they also had four biological children and the temporary kids such as herself who only stayed a few months or years.

The farmhouse was an empty nest now after so many little and not so little feet trampled through it—and through Vicki's heart no doubt. If the walls could speak they would talk of love and caring, compassion, and patience. Everything that was meant to surround a family.

After exchanging pleasantries about the drive over Georgia asked, "Where's Emma? She's not here yet?"

"No, I thought you'd be coming together," Vicki said.

"She wasn't at home when I swung by so I figured she'd already left and driven here on her own."

"Really? That's odd," Vicki said. "Well, come start and if she's late and you eat all the strawberries and clotted cream it's her loss."

They walked into the kitchen where Tom was frying up some ham. The table was laden with enough food for twelve people and there were only the three of them to eat it all.

"You guys do know that I eat in between visits, right? I mean, it looks like you're fattening me up for the slaughter."

"It's habit, Georgie," Tom said. "We've always had so many more people around our table."

"You should see our freezer. It's packed with leftovers." Vicki laughed.

"Where's your sister?" Tom asked as he brought the last tray to the table and they all sat down.

"Can't find her," Georgia said. They all paused the conversation to hold hands and bow their heads. Georgia may eat between visits, but this was definitely the only time she prayed, though she wasn't about to admit that to her very Catholic foster family.

"When did you hear from her last?" Tom asked.

"Yesterday morning," Georgia said around a mouthful of divine roasted potatoes.

"What did she say?" Vicki asked.

"She hasn't been herself lately, Vick. She's swearing like a sailor—I know pot and kettle, but it's just not like her. Her apartment is a mess and all she talks about is her new boyfriend and having sex all the time."

Tom and Vicki glanced at each other with grave concern etched on their faces.

"She's not taking her medication, is she?" Tom asked the rhetorical question.

"She said she's increased her dose, " Georgia said. "But you wouldn't know it. She's almost obsessed with Joe. He's my chief cardiac surgery resident. He's a very smart guy. Driven, on the ball, and he seems to be as taken with her. He called her 'The One.' Things have been crazy at work and I haven't had time to ask him if he's noticed a change. But they've only been together a couple of months."

"If she's fallen for this guy hard enough for him to be obsessing about him and upping her meds then she is on a slippery slope," said Tom. "Her ADHD will have her easily distracted and making impulsive decisions. You know as well as I do, Georgie that she can fall into addictive patterns… sex, drugs, and alcohol. She can start abusing the very medication that makes her well. And she knows this better than we do." It was a pattern they recognized from Emma's rebellious teenage years.

"The other night when I called Joe in on an emergency case, she texted me some nasty threat," Georgia said. "After laying all this out for you, now I'm really getting worried."

"Oh, Tom, we've got to find her and help her." Vicki pushed her untouched food aside.

"We will, Vicki," he said. "We've been through this before. She'll turn up when she's exhausted and hungry. We'll go to her favorite thinking spots and stay at her place today until she comes home if we have to. Then we'll talk some sense into her."

* * *

Matt pedaled harder and wiped the mud spray off his face. No way was number 1158 getting away with both passing him and rooster-tailing mud all over him. He pressed ahead with all his force and passed his opponent. Matt hated second place.

Being out in the fresh air with his friends getting muddy and sweaty was exactly what he needed. If he wanted to stay on the bike and win the race, he had to be in the moment. He couldn't think about all the other stuff going on in his life. He could focus on gears and pedaling, though.

Matt crossed the finish line, beating last year's personal best and everyone he competed with this year. The guys patted him on the back and invited him out for a celebratory beer, but he declined. He'd been focused during the race, but the first thought that came to mind was Georgia and the fact that she wasn't responding to his phone calls or texts.

He walked over to his car, which was sporting four

brand-new tires, and started to towel himself and his bike off and confirmed no response to his texts. Jason—number 1158—walked over, extending a hand. "Sorry about the mud, I hit that puddle at just the right angle, didn't I?"

"Aw, don't worry about it. I can't blame you for trying. You'll have to concede your inability to beat me one day, though." He gave a short laugh.

"I didn't see Ken, he doesn't usually miss this race."

"No, he wasn't here, hey?" Matt did not offer an explanation.

"Well, I'll beat you at the next one, buddy." Jason patted Matt on the shoulder in concession.

"You can try." Matt forced a smile.

Matt climbed into his car, his thoughts consumed with his professional and personal life. Acid burned a hole in his stomach. He was at a complete loss as to who was targeting him and why. This wasn't only about a research study anymore. Ken was dead. They'd worked together, played together, they were friends. Geez, Ken was almost done his thesis and he'd have been a Ph.D. by the fall. What a tragedy. He rested his head on the steering wheel and let a few tears fall while he wondered who called the Liu family and how they were taking it. Should he have been the one to call them? Could he have kept his secret if he did? Matt battled with the crushing sense of feeling responsible for Ken's death. Could he have known the stem cell thief would resort to murder?

He wiped his eyes and started his car. He missed Georgia, longed to hold her and smell her. He wanted her to soften this blow. But she wouldn't answer his calls. It was bad enough that he just lost Ken. Her life had been threatened and not knowing where she was gnawed at him. He had to find her.

* * *

Emma shot back her third long espresso of the hour, trying desperately for a caffeine high. A real high tempted her. She knew where to go to get something stronger. She'd been down that road before. The only thing stopping her was Joe's opinion of her.

But he was in the hospital for the rest of the weekend. Despite this being his weekend off, he chose to work for the extra credit. Since he found out about the only attending position this year, he spent more time with Georgia than he spent with her. Maybe she would go out and find a couple of grams of coke, just to get her through the weekend. Nobody needed to know. She looked up from her cup and as if by divine intervention there were her foster parents and traitorous sister walking through the coffee shop door.

"Hey, Em, you missed brunch," said Miss Perfect Pants with a voice that dripped with honey, but which Emma knew was a total act.

"I was busy," Emma said.

"Mind if we join you for a bit?" Tom asked

"I was actually on my way out."

"Just a few minutes of your time, Emma? We miss you," said Vicki with tenderness in her voice.

"Have it your way." She gestured to an empty chair. Tom and Georgia grabbed two more from a nearby table.

They all sat down like an orchestra. Emma wanted to run. She fidgeted in her seat, eyes trying to catch something in the coffee shop that would hold her interest while these three droned on about missing her lately and asking how was work going and about the new guy she was seeing.

"Emma. Emma?" said Tom.

"What?" These people were so intense. "What do you want from me?"

Tom lowered his voice and tone. "Emma, you've lost control of your ADHD. You're distracted and impulsive and a mess literally and figuratively. You're obsessing over this new man in your life at the expense of everything else."

"You don't know that," she said. "How do you know that my life isn't perfect?" She tucked her hair behind her ear.

"Because Georgia's been to your apartment and we can see it in the way you're sitting here now. This isn't our first rodeo," Tom said.

"Your apartment is a shit pit, Em, I wouldn't let my dog sleep in it," Georgia said.

"Okay, first off, Gus is my fucking dog, not yours," Emma hissed. "And second, I'm not one bit surprised that you'd take her word over mine, Dad. You always have. She's a backstabbing bitch who keeps calling my boyfriend in to work every five minutes just to piss me off."

Vicki started to cry, silent tears falling down the ridges of her slightly wrinkled face. Emma's stomach sank. She hated hurting her mom.

Tom kept his voice low. "Why does Gus live with Georgia?"

"Oh, Christ, you know why," Emma said. She started to spin the spoon on the table to give her something to do with her hand so she wouldn't strangle Georgia.

"Say it," Tom insisted.

"He went to live with her when I was in rehab," Emma said.

"How long have you been playing with your medications and going to meetings?" Tom asked.

"About a month."

"Are you happy with the results?" Tom asked. "Do you

feel healthy, in control of your choices and your life?" She knew the answer to that immediately. What most people didn't realize was that addicts live in a shame spiral. She knew she was out of control, but the effort to pull herself back to reality was overwhelming. As hard as life could be when she high, it was also so easy.

"I was happy when super-surgeon here let me spend time with Joe." Emma wasn't ready to give up yet.

Georgia kept her mouth shut for once and let Tom do all the talking. "Emma, even if your boyfriend worked as a bag boy at the grocery store, he'd have to leave your side eventually. You can't only ever be happy when you're with a guy and not the rest of your life."

"I know that." She crossed her arms.

They all sat in silence for a few minutes. Emma scratched at her arm. She needed to leave the scrutiny. It just added to the shame spiral.

"Emma, why don't you come home with us and we can get you settled back into your medication and self-care routine?"

"Joe doesn't know I have all this shit going on in my life and I want to get off these meds and learn to live without them so I can get pregnant one day." That truth slipped out of her mouth and was a surprise to even herself.

"You can't possibly be talking about having kids now? He hasn't finished residency," Georgia cut in again.

"We haven't gotten around to discussing it yet," Emma said.

"Well, we three know you the best in the whole world," Tom said, "and we know how well you can be, and how happy and fulfilled your life is when you take your meds, when you practice your mindfulness, when you go to yoga. There's lots of time to find a way to have your ADHD under control and start a family. Right now, we need to get you well again before you go looking for a drug dealer. It's a razor's edge when you're in this state."

"Come home with us, baby girl," Vicki said and she held Emma's hand. Her gentle grip was so soft. And comforting. She suddenly couldn't stop the torrent of tears and fell into Vicki's hug.

Chapter 13

"For the love of Christ! What do you want? This has got to be your seventh call today!" Georgia yelled into her cell phone as she stood in the disarray that was Emma's apartment.

"Thank God you finally answered. Are you all right? Are you safe?" Matt said, sounding breathless.

"I'm busy with the rest of my life."

"What can be more pressing than a threat against your life and a dying patient?"

"Housekeeping, apparently," Georgia said.

"Georgia, I need to see you, to talk to you," Matt said. "The last time we spoke, things were left hanging. You know, elephant in the room kind of things."

Georgia put on a pair of rubber gloves she kept in her purse in case of medical emergencies and started on the most pressing garbage she needed out of her line of sight. "Matt, I'm not sure now is the best time for us to have serious conversations. My life is pretty much a pile of shit. And I'm up to my eyeballs in condoms and lube."

"Excuse me?"

"Listen, my foster sister is having a hard time, and while she's with the family getting better, I'm cleaning her apartment."

"Can I come over and help?" Matt asked.

Why? Why did she long to say "yes" with every cell in her body? Man, she wanted to hate him. And at the same time, she wanted to be with him every waking minute. She started to wonder if there was something in the air in

Emma's apartment to make them all so love-drunk. She opened the window.

"Georgia? You still there?"

"Yes."

"Okay, what's the address?"

"No, I meant, 'yes I'm still here.'"

"Where?" Matt pressed.

"Good God, you are the most annoying thing alive. 596 Warren Street."

"I'll be right there." He sounded downright giddy.

"Bring some rubber gloves and some bleach."

She continued to tidy up the bedroom, throwing the bedding and every piece of clothing that was on the floor into the washing machine. She would try to have the bedroom presentable before Matt arrived—no need to embarrass Emma.

By the time Matt showed up, all that was left were the bathroom and kitchen. She gave Matt the toilet brush and set him to work.

Unfortunately, the apartment was small enough to actually hold a conversation.

"So, what's up with your foster sister?" he said from toilet scrubbing duty.

"I guess you wouldn't cross paths with her at the hospital. Don't let this mess fool you. She's a pretty amazing child psychologist and usually leads an exemplary, but kind of boring, life. She's recently had a relapse of ADHD."

"Forgive my ignorance, but why would that be an issue?" he said. "Doesn't that just make it hard for her to concentrate?"

"No. She was born to a drug-addicted mother. ADHD is the label our foster family likes to use for many of her issues. Impulsiveness, addictions, obsessions," Georgia explained. "Our foster parents spent a lot of years finding solutions to all her issues, and she's great if she stays on her regimen of medication, meditation, and exercise. But she fell in love and forgot the risks of quitting what works."

"And one of her symptoms is poor housekeeping?"

"Among other things," Georgia said. "I think she's been obsessing about sex, falling into an addictive pattern. I honestly think it could have been mere days before she was on the streets with a hypodermic needle hanging out of her arm."

"Wow, that's serious," he said. "And meditation helped enough for her to be in charge of children's mental health?"

"Surprisingly enough, combined with everything else." There was relatively little to do in the kitchen once the takeout containers were all thrown out and the dishes and counter were washed. Georgia wiped down the inside of the fridge, which was empty save for a bottle of ketchup and some pickles.

The dryer buzzed the end of a cycle and she headed to the washroom to fetch the sheets to make the bed. Matt stood from scrubbing the bathtub and turned to her. What a vision, Matt: the sexiest man she'd ever set eyes on, his broad shoulders filling a charcoal cashmere sweater, and him sporting yellow rubber gloves. He returned her smile and it crinkled his eyes, sparking a glow of heat in her chest.

"You wear the Molly Maid look very well. The yellow in the gloves brings out the blue of your eyes," she said.

"Thank you." He took off the gloves and washed his hands while Georgia emptied the dry clothes into a basket. She took the sheets into the bedroom and started making the bed. Matt followed and helped from the other side.

"It looks like we're pretty much done," he said. "Can I take you out for dinner so we can sit and talk?"

Georgia sighed. "I'm not going to escape this talking business, now am I?"

"Please?"

"Well, since you're begging." She laughed and before she knew it, he had crawled across the bed and flipped her over. He tickled her to roaring laughter with tears streaming down her face. She managed to take the top position and straddled him, pinning his hands on either side of his head. The sight was more than she could bear and she leaned in for a long passionate kiss. His tongue was becoming familiar and the sensation of it teasing hers sent shivers up her spine. Her nipples responded, rubbing against the lace of her bra and she soon noticed an erection pressing against her aching groin.

She pulled away and got up off the bed, not ready to forgive completely just yet. "Let's get out of here. I'm hungry. Italian?" She finished making the bed without making eye contact. First, she wasn't ready to go that far again with Matt, they did need to talk. And second, she sure as hell didn't want to have sex in Emma's apartment after all the stuff she found today.

"Are you kidding? My name is Mancini."

"Oh, yeah. Know any good restaurants then?"

"Buongiorno's is owned by my uncle," he said. "They'll treat us like royalty. You'll be lucky to leave with your pants still done up."

Taking her pants off was exactly what she was trying to avoid.

* * *

Georgia's stomach growled as soon as they sat down at their table. The bread arrived and she scarfed down half the loaf. Matt's uncle appeared with a fabulous bottle of wine made from a grape Georgia had never heard of and was soon followed by his research nurse Judy, who she remembered also happened to be his cousin. They all rose to do the customary kiss on both cheeks, then Judy helped herself to a chair and joined them. Uninvited.

"What's happening in the lab, Matt? I mean, first the money is an issue, then there are locks installed all over the place, then Ken doesn't show up for work today. I know embryonic stem cells used to be a censorious subject, but why all the mystery lately?" Judy's hands flew as she spoke, showing off the Italian in her. Georgia stared at Matt's face across the table and decided she wanted some Italian in her too.

Matt gave an avoidance response, changing the subject to one no Italian mother could ever ignore. He asked about her kids. Well, that conversation lasted through most of the main course. Luckily, Georgia was hungry enough to not care about having to share Matt while listening to Manny's little escapade of flushing Nona's glasses down the toilet.

Finally, when dessert arrived, Judy caught on to her third-wheel status and left. A third glass of wine was poured for Georgia. She'd noticed Matt had stopped at one glass.

"So, how was your day, honey?" Georgia said, grinning. She knew there was something more serious she wanted to talk about but the wine softened the edges off every topic she could think of.

"Great. I won the cyclocross race again this year," he said as he stirred sugar into his cappuccino.

"You cycle? Competitively?"

"I do everything competitively." He smiled a sexy grin that suggested a double entendre.

"That explains your tantalizing gluteus maximus."

Matt licked the foam off his upper lip. She kept her eyes on his tongue. "I would advise against teasing me with that tongue in public, doctor. You don't want me climbing over this table in your uncle's restaurant, do you?"

Matt raised his hand at the server close by. "Check, please."

* * *

Matt drove them to her place. He got out of his car and walked around to her side, opening the door for her. Usually, she'd be annoyed by a man thinking she couldn't open her own damn door, but after claiming most of that bottle of wine for herself, she actually did need help with the damn door. She stood and gave him a gentle kiss on his cheek. "Thank you, sir. Won't you come upstairs for a nightcap?"

"Well, maybe a coffee." He took her hand in his and opened the main door to the building. The doorman stood quickly as they approached.

"Dr. Laurence, good evening."

"Hi, Fred."

"Um, Dr. Laurence," he continued as they walked past to the elevator, "You received a parcel late this afternoon. The delivery man insisted on leaving it on your doorstep and not with me. But I assure you, I've been making sure it's right where he left it."

"Thanks, Fred."

Once inside the elevator, Georgia slinked over to Matt and stuck her hand up his shirt rubbing his chest as she kissed his jaw and neck. The wine made her forget anything she had needed to be angry about.

They made their way to her apartment door, almost tripping over a small box because they were intertwined in their kiss. Georgia let go of him long enough to dig out her keys and Matt picked up the package. The bottom was wet.

"You'd better open this now, babe," he said. "I think it's leaking, whatever it is."

They walked through the door and a happy Gus met them, tail wagging like a metronome set to allegro. As soon as Gus smelled the box in Matt's hands, he sat and begged with a paw up.

"This isn't a doggy bag from dinner, fella." Matt put the box on the kitchen counter and walked to the sink to wash his now sticky hands. The soap lathered pink.

"That's odd. I'm not expecting anything." She sliced open the top of the box, peered inside, and turned away. "Oh my God."

Matt looked inside. It was a heart punctured through with a butcher knife. A note was taped to the side of the box.

"You are spending too much time with the enemy."

Chapter 14

"Stay right here, Georgia. Let me check around the rest of the apartment to make sure they didn't come in," Matt said, his panic audible.

"I'm coming with you. You won't know if anything's missing." Georgia grabbed his bicep and followed him.

"They weren't here for your TV and jewelry, Georgia. They wanted to scare you."

"It's working." Her heart roared in her ears as she tried to slow down her breathing. They held hands and walked through the condo. Nothing was missing.

"Get yourself an overnight bag," Matt said. "You're not staying here tonight."

"But they don't want us together. That's what the note meant. And how do we know you don't have the same package at your place?" Georgia said.

"We don't. But I'm not leaving your side, I don't care what the note says," Matt said. "Besides, I live in a gated community, and I know that a package would never be left on my doorstep. We need to sit down and think and look at our options. We need to get someone to investigate this who will be discreet and not cost us the research. I'm going to contact my dad's private investigator."

Georgia grabbed a few personal items and some clothes for the office the next day. "I'm not leaving Gus here. Does your fancy community allow dogs?"

"Yes." He ignored the dig, and Georgia immediately regretted it. Her nerves were frayed. This whole week had been exhausting her usual reserve of calm. She typically leaned toward the fight part of fight or flight, even though her weapons were usually just words. This running away to hide business threw her for a loop.

"I'll grab his leash and food and bowls from the kitchen," Matt said, "and you stick the heart in the fridge, we'll need it for evidence once we find this son of a bitch."

* * *

They drove up to a gate seemingly in the middle of nowhere and Matt got out of the car to talk to the gatekeeper. He came back and announced, "No one left anything for me, and they've been alerted to pay extra attention for a while." He continued down a winding path with mature trees and stellar homes about two hundred feet apart.

"Nice neighborhood. I guess the gangs tag their graffiti in gold, eh?" Georgia giggled.

"Oh, we don't have any gang activity around here."

"I was kidding, jackass." She smiled and he put his hand on her knee, removing it only once he made a sharp turn into his driveway.

They drove up to a stunning Victorian house, or, rather, a modern version of a Victorian. It had obviously been built within the last five years. The lawns and English garden were immaculate and the flagstone path that led from the detached triple door garage was lined with small lanterns to guide their way. Gus wasted no time whizzing on one of them.

"Wow, these are some digs you've got here," Georgia said. She remembered the kind of luxury Phil enjoyed back when she dated him. She had always paid her way, wouldn't even let him buy her a drink at the club. No way was anyone going to accuse her of sniffing around the Mancinis for money. Phil had been her first love, but it was fleeting and immature, an escape from the grueling grind of medical school. Matt was something completely different. He was comfort, stability, safety, and made this current terrifying reality more bearable. Maybe she'd grown up a bit since med school.

Matt turned the lock, opened the door, and keyed in his code on the security system. "Welcome to my home."

Gus ran past them, sniffed around a couple of rooms, and found his spot on a loveseat.

"Go ahead, Gus, make yourself at home," said Georgia, wishing she had the simple life of a dog right now.

"Let me show you around," Matt said. He led the way, pointing out his study to the left of the foyer, the formal living room where Gus had decided to live was to their left, and a staircase straight ahead. The hall then led to a chef's kitchen. "You cook?" Georgia asked.

"When I get the chance. Something to drink?" Matt asked.

"Water, please."

He grabbed two bottles of water and resumed the tour. The rear of the house was made of three sets of French doors leading to an outdoor eating area, living area, and inground pool. They continued on to pass a television room and a formal dining room, which lead them back to the stairs.

"I have two guest rooms if you'd rather some privacy tonight," Matt said as he lead the way to the second floor.

"Thanks, but the last thing I need is to be in a strange bed, in a strange house, alone, after having my life threatened again."

"I'd be honored to be your comfort and protection tonight," he said, placing a hand on his heart.

Matt opened the double doors to the master bedroom and a subtle whiff of his natural aroma tickled her nose. She realized at that moment that though they'd already had sex and spent most of the week in each other's company, walking into his bedroom was the most intimate she'd been with him. Matt Mancini had slipped into her life without her knowledge and now she felt like a rock enveloped by the roots of an enormous oak. Safe and surrounded by an undying love, something she hadn't allowed herself to feel since her mom died, despite her foster family's best efforts.

She sat on the bench at the foot of the bed and turned her chin up and offered Matt her most sensual smile. He took the bait and her mouth in his. The sensation of his kiss piqued the desire barely hiding beneath her surface and soon Georgia lost all thought processes as his hands explored her starving body. He lifted her off the bench and onto the long dresser to face him. His mouth didn't leave hers until it descended her throat toward the swell of her breast. He adeptly liberated her from her bra and shirt. Georgia's body ached with hunger for his as she tugged up her skirt, underwear down, and unzipped his pants.

Matt entered her as she wrapped her legs around his hips and her arms around his neck, fusing to him in a torrent of passion. He lowered his mouth to meet her nipples where he lingered making her arc her back in delight. He lifted her to the bed where he placed her hips on a pillow and found the perfect rhythm that had them both reach the pinnacle of release. Georgia threw her head back as sparks of light filled her vision and her body shuddered with pleasure. She held on tighter, burying her face in Matt's neck as he panted in her ear while they both returned to equilibrium.

* * *

Georgia got the call at six in the morning that Ms. Jenkins' vitals were headed south. The protocols that Dr. Childs had provided didn't cover the scenarios Ms. Jenkins was presenting. Both she and Matt dressed and rushed to the hospital.

The sky pinked as the sun rose over the horizon when they pulled into the parking lot. Matt went straight to his office to make a high priority call to the best private investigator his family money could buy, which reassured her ethics and their safety. Georgia ran up the stairs two by two in the direction of the SICU.

She found a quiet calm at the nurses' station. Most of the other patients were ready to transfer to the wards to clear up space for the Monday operations, none of which she would be performing. But there was plenty of activity in room three. Joe stood at the head of the bed with a 7.5 endotracheal tube while a respiratory tech keyed the pressure setting into the respirator. Meanwhile, Shawna slept soundly in an armchair in the corner.

"What's she doing here?" Georgia whispered.

"Her aunt had guys over at the apartment doing drugs at the kitchen table, so she came here at two in the morning," Joe explained.

"Oh, Christ."

"The night shift nurse coordinator called social services when she found her here."

"What!" Georgia said.

"Hey, uh, Dr. L? Mind giving me a clue what you want to be done once she's intubated? Her PO2 is in her boots," Joe said.

"Let me see her numbers and somebody call Dr. Childs."

"We did, it's an answering machine. Says he's on vacation," replied Brian.

"You have got to be kidding me," Georgia said. "Call the hospital and have them call his cell. I don't care if he's on Waikiki Beach, I want to talk to him now."

Georgia took the lab sheets to the nurses' station for better light. The nurse there was placing phone calls but was clearly on hold. "When you have a minute, I'd give a king's ransom for a coffee, two cream, two sugar," Georgia said.

By the horrified look on the nurse's face, Georgia deduced that she was one of those nurses who believed she was above fetching coffee for a doctor.

"This isn't about ego or hierarchy. I promise," Georgia said. "It's for the benefit of the patient's care. I'll think better." She plastered on a smile for the nurse if it meant she'd get a cup of coffee sooner.

The lab numbers sucked. Georgia shook her head. What was this woman surviving on? She leaned forward and rubbed her face with both hands. She had no choice. It was back to the balloon pump for Ms. Jenkins.

"After you get a hold of Dr. Childs, can you call Carol and have her come in?" Georgia said.

"Would that be before or after I fetch you a coffee, Dr. Laurence?"

"Before, please."

If only this nurse understood that her requests had nothing to do with her gender or title as a nurse but Georgia's single-mindedness for helping Ms. Jenkins and her reliance on her team. But she also didn't have the energy to explain that right now.

She walked into the room where Joe was staring up at the heart monitor. "Every time we increase the PEEP on the ventilator her heart rate drops," he said.

"We're going to put the balloon pump back in," Georgia said.

"Did you talk to Dr. Childs already?"

"No. Our other option is to wait two hours and watch this woman die." Georgia grabbed Joe's stethoscope from around his neck and listened to Ms. Jenkins' lungs to make sure the intubation was done right and to listen for the distinct murmur at the apex of her heart.

"I'll round up the equipment," Joe said.

As Joe walked out of the room, he was replaced by a linebacker-sized older lady.

"I'm Betty Thompson from social services, here to collect Shawna Jenkins." Her posh English accent gave her an air of condescension and set Georgia's hackles up immediately. Shawna's face mixed with sleep, bewilderment, and fear as she figured out what was going on around her.

"Yeah, actually, that was all a misunderstanding," Georgia said as she palpated the swelling in Ms. Jenkins' ankles. "I'm Dr. Georgia Laurence, chief of cardiac surgery here at Our Lady of Grace, and in my opinion, Shawna doesn't need to be placed. Ms. Jenkins will be out of the woods in a few days. If you are not happy with her current arrangements, then Shawna can stay with me."

Brian started waving from the corner of the room. "Um, Dr. Laurence... She's decelerating real quick over here."

"Fucking shit!" Georgia ran to the head of the bed and felt for a pulse. "She needs that balloon pump, let's go!"

Georgia slipped into a sterile gown and donned a set of sterile gloves as a nurse uncovered Ms. Jenkins' right clavicle and spread down a sterile field. Georgia was swabbing the area with iodine and mapping out her landmarks for the insertion of the subclavian arterial line when she noticed Betty leading Shawna out of the room.

"Hey, where are you taking her?" Georgia called out.

"I'm sorry Dr. Laurence, I'm sure your credentials as a surgeon are stellar, but there are myriad reasons why Shawna cannot stay with you, including a marked conflict of interest considering you are Ms. Jenkins' caregiver. Shawna should not be here to witness this procedure performed on her mom. Evidently, Ms. Jenkins is in no way ready to go home and you, ma'am, have the potty mouth of a merchant marine."

"Shawna, I'll make sure you're well taken care of, I promise, but right now I have to fix your mom, so I can't sort this out until later. Go to school and I'll catch up with you later," Georgia said.

"If Mom wakes up tell her I love her," Shawna said through the thickness of tears. It tore at Georgia more than she thought possible but she pushed the feeling down.

"Will do." Georgia turned to the rest of the staff in the room. "Okay, let's get this woman's heart pumping again."

Chapter 15

Matt sat at his desk and stared at the ceiling, steeling his resolve. He hated the prospect of calling his brother, but he could think of no one else who would have access to his father's contact lists. He needed the best private investigator money could buy and he knew the only place to find someone to fit that bill would be a recommendation from his dad. But his father would ask too many questions and judge every possible scenario Matt would offer.

He used his landline to ensure Phil would pick-up. "Dr. Phillip Mancini."

"Hey, Phil. It's Matt. I need a favor."

"Well, I'll be damned. If it isn't my brother calling to ask me for something," said Phil, dripping in scorn. "I never thought I'd live to see the day."

"Yeah, yeah. Listen, this is urgent and important, so no screwing around. I need you to dip into Dad's Rolodex for his private investigator."

"How do you know Dad has a private investigator?" Phil asked.

"I saw him use one a few times. Last time was to investigate your ex-fiancée, remember?"

"So what are you calling me for? Why don't you call Dad?"

Matt should have known it wouldn't have been any easier to get anything from Phil without stroking his ego in the process. "Listen, I'm sorry, I'm on edge. I told you it was urgent, I don't have time for twenty questions." He started to tidy up the mess around him, then stopped and thought maybe the private investigator would want to see the crime scene. It was hard to believe that his own office was an actual crime scene.

"I get one more. Why do you need a PI?" Phil asked.

"None of your damned business. Are you going to give me the number or not?"

"I don't know. It sounds pretty important. Urgent you said."

"For the love of God. I didn't call Dad first because you're always attached at the hip anyway. But if you prefer that I tell him you gave me the runaround and suggested I waste his precious time I'll just hang up and call him instead."

"I'll transfer you to my assistant, she's got the Rolodex in her filing cabinet."

"Thanks." Matt's attempt at gratitude was cut off by the phone line being transferred. Luckily, Phil's assistant was much easier and more pleasant to deal with. He had the name and number within seconds.

Before dialing, he did an internet search on the name. The guy didn't exist as far as Google was concerned. Typical of his father to use some dark web, stealth PI to check out a future daughter-in-law.

He dialed the number and a sandpaper voice replied, "Yes."

"This is Dr. Matt Mancini. You did some work for my dad in the past."

"Yes."

"I need something investigated. Can we meet to discuss it in person?"

"What you need investigated?"

"A crime." Matt could be as cagey as the PI guy.

"The cops involved?" the scratchy voiced asked.

"Only partly. They can't be told the full story yet."

"You do something wrong?"

"No." Matt tried to not sound offended.

"I'll meet you where the crime was perpetrated and we will discuss my fees in person."

* * *

Once Ms. Jenkins was settled on the balloon pump, and the night shift, including an exhausted Brian and Joe, had gone home, Georgia went to her office to call her lawyer Stuart to see what could be done to get Shawna back. He agreed to come right over. In the meantime, not having heard anything, Georgia called Carol to check on the transplant front.

"Hey, Carol, are you avoiding me?"

"No, we had a crazy weekend. All those motor vehicle accidents really drum up business."

"None of them with ancestors from a tiny little area in southwest Africa carrying the Duffy negative antibodies we need?" Georgia pleaded.

"No. I'm sorry, Georgia."

"Well, I thought I'd tell you she's on the balloon pump at the moment. I couldn't attach an LVAD. She'll die before the end of the week if we don't get a heart."

"She's the only one on our list with that blood type. She gets the next one that comes along countrywide."

"Thanks." Georgia hung up.

She wasn't the praying type, but at this point, she was considering a bath in holy water and lighting every candle in the hospital chapel. So many things were going wrong in her life. If God was listening, she hoped he would take out a heart donor so she could save Sandra Jenkins.

Georgia's assistant Diane knocked on the door, waking her from her pity party. "Come in."

Georgia stood when her lawyer followed her assistant into the office. "Thanks for coming, Stuart."

"I'm happy to get to talk to you in person," he said. "I got a call from the hospital lawyers with a rundown of everything. You are in some hot water." Stuart settled into the chair across her desk and pulled out a legal pad.

"Oh, you're talking about Mrs. Reynolds' death."

"Why else would I be here?"

"I wanted you to help me place a patient's daughter into foster care with my old foster parents," Georgia said.

"You do know you are being sued for wrongful death." Stuart cocked his head in disbelief at Georgia's priorities.

Georgia waved away the invisible pest. "That's just a threat."

"No. It's not. The hospital is not letting you operate because they are afraid of this lawsuit. Mr. Reynolds is extremely angry. He's gone and hired himself the best ambulance chaser in town."

"For now, I have other things to deal with."

"You don't seem to understand. You can lose your medical license. You will never practice medicine again if you lose this case," Stuart said.

The fire in her gut competed with the tears that threatened to fall. She wanted to punch something so bad. "But I don't even know what the hell happened!"

"Then you should be very scared. I will do everything I possibly can, but first I need you to take things a little more seriously, Georgia. You and I both know that you have a tendency to run off at the mouth. This is not the time."

"What do we need to do then?"

"We need those autopsy reports, pronto," Stuart said.

"I'll send Diane down to stand over their shoulder until we get the results. She'll bring them up to me." Georgia pressed the intercom button and gave her assistant her orders.

"Once we have those, you and I are going to sit and

have a very long talk about everything that went on in that OR from the time you walked through the doors to the time you called the death in the SICU." He pulled out another file folder from his bag. "There's one other matter I need to discuss with you. It seems that a nurse, Marion Hammon, is contesting an incident report you filed about her. Seriously, Georgia, is there anyone you haven't angered this week?"

"Oh, for fuck's sake, that clumsy merchant of death!" Georgia said, boiling over. "I stand by every word in that incident report and will spend my last dime defending it. I'll testify in court if I have to." As if she didn't have enough to deal with. That hateful excuse for a nurse could rot in hell. She pushed up from her desk and started to pace her office, realizing for the first time how small it was and how few steps it took to walk the length of the room. "Now, while we wait for those reports and for everyone I've pissed off to burn me at the stake, can you do anything about Shawna Jenkins being placed into foster care with my foster parents?"

"Why? With everything going on, why do you need to play God with Shawna in the foster care system?" he asked.

"To ensure she's well taken care of. I was trying my best to avoid her being placed into the system at all, but if she has to be in it, I want her with Tom and Vicki."

"I'll see what I can do."

Chapter 16

Emma put away the dishes from the drainboard while Vicki rolled out some pie crust on the island behind the sink. She'd spent many evenings trading with the other kids in this house to dry instead of washing the dishes after dinner when she was growing up. They all seemed to love the bubbly water, but she much preferred to keep her hands dry.

"I can't believe how good you look this afternoon, dear. Are you feeling any better?" Vicki said.

"A bit. Well enough to notice the contrast to how awful I felt last week, and I just kept making it worse," Emma said. "I don't know how I could be so stupid. The first guy to come along and show me some attention, I lose myself." Emma folded the cloth and hung it on the stove.

"There's a very good reason for the old saying 'love is blind,'" said Vicki. "Because it is. You're not stupid. You want someone to share your life with, there's nothing wrong with that. You need to go slow with it. The same way you generally have to go slow with all your decisions. That's one of the first things we taught you as a kid—once we knew what was going on—that you're as good as anyone out there, you just need to remind yourself to take a little more time making your choices and decisions to make the right ones for you."

If only Vicki knew how awful her choices had been over the last month and how close she had been to making a very, very bad one the day they walked into the coffee shop.

"I take that back," Emma said. "I didn't lose everything the first time. I never lost you guys. My family that will do anything for me to be healthy. I'm so grateful for everything you've ever done for me." Emma gave Vicki a hug. Vicki, notoriously close to tears at the drop of a hat, pulled a tissue out of her sleeve to dry her eyes.

"I think I'll give Joe a call and explain things to him, in case he's wondering where I am."

"You sure you're up for that already?"

"I know I'm not ready to run over and spend the afternoon with him if that's what you mean. I owe it to him to be truthful about where I am and what I'm doing and the truth about my mental health if there is going to be any future for us."

Emma walked upstairs to her old room. It had become a guest room once she'd moved out after college. The walls were painted a nice taupe green instead of the flashy purple and a zillion posters of P!nk and No Doubt. She dug her cell phone out of her purse. It was dead. She plugged it into the wall and saw that she'd missed four calls from Joe. The last one was an hour ago. He must have gotten off work. The one thing she'd longed for, Joe to have a day off, and now she knew better than to spend it in bed with him.

She picked up her old landline phone in the shape of pink lips—not everything in her room had been replaced. A sleepy Joe answered.

"I'm waking you up, I'm so sorry."

"Emma? Where the hell are you? I've been calling for two days now. I asked Dr. L where you were, and she gave me a non-answer."

"I'm at my old foster home. I'm with my family." She corrected herself.

"Why? What's wrong?"

"Joe, I haven't been completely honest with you about my mental health," she said. Then the rest came pouring out. "A lot of it comes from my biological mom being a drug addict. Studies are just now looking into all the correlations between ADHD and addiction and trauma. There's so much more involved in my mental health than inattention. I relapsed in my sobriety, to some degree, by trying to hide things from you and I was getting worse and—"

"Wait a minute," Joe cut in. "You're fine, Emma. Who's filling your head with this relapse bullshit?"

"Joe, I think I was getting addicted to you, and to sex with you."

"That's a problem?" He laughed.

"It is when it consumes your whole life," she said slightly hurt from his reaction. How much she would have loved for it to not be a problem. "I wasn't taking care of myself or my apartment or my job or my friendships and family."

"Sounds to me like this is some crap a friend put in your head because you were spending more time with me than them," he said more forcefully than she'd ever heard him speak before.

"I've known myself for thirty-one years. I know my body and I know my mind and I know what works best to make me better. I'm doing what I know works. If you can't accept me taking a bit of a breather, then you can't have me in your life." Emma surprised herself with her determination, but once the words came out, she knew they were her truth. Mental health was her whole existence. Championing other people's mental health and caring for her own. She couldn't risk allowing it to slip away for anyone's sake.

"Baby, come on, don't talk like that. I love you, you know it," Joe pleaded.

"Then let me heal. When I'm better, I'll call you, and we can have a real good heart to heart."

"But I miss you," he said, his tone softening, enticing. "I want you lying here beside me right now. I'm so tired. I need you. Here. With me."

"I can't come today. I'll see you soon." She hung up before he could say anything else that would draw her to him.

She wanted to go be with him. Her body ached to be held close to his. She hated being well enough to know she was being ruled by impulses, yet still having those longings raking her body.

She started to fear that Joe would ever be able to accept her for who she was. There was something in his voice.

Emma mentally re-examined their time together and realized that he had behaved differently over the last few weeks. Dinner dates at nice restaurants had become takeout. Evening walks holding hands were replaced with sex on her couch. They even stopped going on hikes, something she'd loved. Her clinical psychology background started kicking in and drummed up all kinds of scenarios, none of them pretty. Then she stopped herself, recognizing that she was trying to pin their relationship issues on him. She played her part. She had enough issues for the two of them and then some.

She needed more time to heal, but she would heal. She'd been successful before she could do it again.

* * *

Georgia walked into Matt's office and threw the autopsy report onto his desk.

"It looks like it's my career or your study, lover boy. Because this autopsy says we've just been fucked with a sixteen-inch-long dildo."

"Dr. Laurence, this is Vince Delgatto, the PI I've hired for us," Matt said.

How could she have missed an imposing figure like Vince when she walked into the room? Taking all of him in, she was struck by both his unremarkable features and distinct don't-fuck-with-me persona.

"Now that's my kind of broad," Vince spoke with a

thick Bronx accent and stuck out a beefy hand with sausages for fingers.

"Yeah, well, you'd better be the kind of investigator that can dig us out of a huge pile of shit," Georgia said.

Matt grabbed the report and scanned it to the juicy part, then read aloud: "The findings are consistent with an injection of a cell enhancing substance such as human growth hormones or stem cells. Cause of death is not related to the growth of new tissue, however, the patient exsanguinated from anticoagulants preventing the closure of the puncture wound in the left ventricle."

"In English, please," Vince said, leaning in.

"Whoever stole the cells stuck them into Mrs. Reynolds' heart," Georgia translated. "The hole made her bleed to death because I had her on medication to stop her blood from clotting on her new metallic valve." She turned to Matt and spat out, "I'm regretting the day I walked into this office looking for help. My patients are dying, and I've gotten nothing out of this but death threats."

Vince pulled out a pad and pen. "Who all was in the operating room with you that day?" he said.

"It couldn't have been in the OR. I inspected the heart before I closed up. Dr. Joe Carter, my chief resident, was worried that he nicked the heart, so I checked it before closing, there wasn't a mark on the heart. Then I did the closing."

"Georgia, it had to have been in the OR. You just didn't see the hole," Matt said.

"You're going to sit there and tell me—me—that I made a mistake?" she spat out. Was she wrong to trust another full-of-himself Mancini? The nerve of the guy! "I didn't make chief of cardiac surgery on my good looks, asshole. I know what I'm doing in an OR. My career is only going down the tubes because of you and your goddamned stem cells, and this fucking research that we have to save at all costs. Well, the price is getting a little too high for me." She thought of Shawna, and Ms. Jenkins, of herself and all the patients she could be helping if she could still operate, and of everything her lawyer had spelled out for her.

"Give Vince the names of who was in the operating room and he'll do his job. Then you can deliver the killer and your autopsy report to the board and be in the OR tomorrow," Matt said. She knew he was trying to reassure her, but it did little good.

"Fine," she said, relenting slightly. "Vince, meet me in my office where I have access to the chart through my computer. I'll give you the names of the people who took care of her immediately post-op too. And when we're in the clear for this shit, we're going to have a conversation about implying that I don't know what goes on under my nose during surgery, Matt."

"Actually, Dr. Laurence, I also want to have a look around your apartment and the package you'd been sent," Vince said.

"I'll give you the keys and my address when you come to my office."

She turned to leave and Matt grabbed her arm. "Vince, mind having a peek at that refrigerator again? I want to talk to Georgia for a second."

Georgia faced him. "Why, so you can tell me I don't know what I'm doing in my own OR again? You want to make it worse and tell me I'm horrible in bed too?"

"We're both under a lot of stress and we're saying things we don't mean. You're a fantastic surgeon and the best sex I've ever had. Let Vince find this guy. I'm going to call California and ask for the go-ahead to use Ms. Jenkins for a human trial. We just need to keep all of this mess from them until we find out who is sabotaging the study. I promise."

"Your promise means nothing unless you can make time stand still. Vince had better be a bigger miracle maker than you and I could ever hope for." Georgia turned and walked out.

Chapter 17

Georgia left her office soon after she'd briefed Vince and tried Tom and Vicki's number again on her cell as she took the stairs down to SICU. Finally, the busy signal stopped and it rang. Vicki answered.

"Why on Earth don't you guys get call waiting? I've been trying to call for-fucking-ever."

"Excuse me? Emma was on the phone with her boyfriend." Vicki was curt, she didn't like it when Georgia cussed.

"I'm sorry, I'm having a day from hell. Can you get Tom to pick up the other line? I have an emergency favor." Georgia stopped in the stairwell and leaned on the cold brick of the wall. She needed to ground herself, take a deep breath, and calm down.

"Tom, it's Georgia, pick up the line, it's an emergency," Vicki said.

"Hi, Georgia. What's wrong?" Tom said, joining the call.

"I need you guys to do everything you can to get my patient's daughter into your care. Her name is Shawna Jenkins. I can't remember the social worker's name… English accent, built like a brick house. Betty something?"

"Betty Thompson. The strictest social worker you'll ever have to deal with in your lifetime," Tom offered.

"Yeah, that's her," Georgia said. "I also called my lawyer to try to get them to award you temporary custody."

"Georgia, we haven't taken in kids for years now," Tom said. "We retired when you guys all graduated. I don't know if they'll let us have her. Certainly not permanently."

"Tom, you have to do this. For me. This kid is me when I was young. Her mom is her everything. Her mom has worked so hard to get them stability and I don't want to lose Shawna to a string of broken homes and abuse. It's only until I fix up Ms. Jenkins. Please, Tom? Vicki?"

"Let's go downtown to the office, Tom. We can get her. I'm Betty's favorite, she'll do this for me." Vicki had a heart of gold and could never watch a fly suffer, let alone a girl in need.

"Oh, thank you, thank you, thank you. I love you guys." Georgia started back down the stairs and into the SICU corridor.

"We love you too. We'll call you when she's here," Tom said.

One phone call accomplished. Georgia stepped up to the heart monitors at the nurses' station and pulled up Ms. Jenkins' labs while she dialed Dr. Childs. The labs were not improving this time, despite the balloon pump.

Dr. Childs finally picked up the phone after Georgia was transferred three times.

"It's about time. Are you avoiding my calls again, Bruce?"

"No. I'm a busy man, that's all."

"Well, your shit doesn't work. Ms. Jenkins is spiraling down the toilet in a hurry. I had to put her on the balloon pump this morning and her labs aren't getting any better."

"My medication is not the problem. Your patient is dying. I told you it's never been used on someone that sickly. You need to face that fact. There's nothing anyone can do for her," Bruce said.

"That's all you've got for me? Your best advice is to give up? What kind of loser gives up?"

"How soon you fall out of love, Dr. Laurence. A short while ago you thought I walked on water. There are no miracles here. This is science."

"Thanks for your words of wisdom, Plato. Have a nice

life." She hung up the phone just as the alarms started chiming on the heart monitor in Ms. Jenkins' room.

Georgia was ready to surge into action, but the nurses and respiratory therapist were already reacting flawlessly to get Ms. Jenkins' vitals to stabilize. She resorted to standing at the head of the bed and whispering into her ear.

"Sandra, it's Dr. Laurence. Listen. We need you to fight this. Shawna needs you. I know you're tired, but we're going to get you some relief very soon. Keep up the fight for your daughter."

The heart monitor showed some improvements. Though very slight, they were enough to keep the damned thing from ringing. Georgia stood but kept her hand on Ms. Jenkins while she asked the nurse to page Dr. Mancini and call Joe to come in early.

"Dr. Laurence, he's only been gone for eight hours," the charge nurse said.

"Resident's don't have the same collective agreement as nurses. Eight hours is plenty of sleep. He's the best right-hand man I've got. All the other residents are taking care of my more stable patients right now."

She leaned down to Ms. Jenkins' ear again. "I know you're wondering where Shawna is because it's after supper time. She's with my mom." Georgia embellished the truth a bit, "I'm making sure she's well-fed and taken care of. As soon as my mom can, she'll bring her by to visit."

Georgia had never, ever called Vicki her mom. The word was sacred to her and only belonged to one woman in her life. Yet, she was sure it was the most comforting and trustworthy word for Ms. Jenkins to hear. She also had to admit that it comforted her own heart too.

"Dr. Mancini is on his way down. Joe said he'll be here as soon as he's had a shit, shower, and shave—his words, not mine," the nurse said.

Chapter 18

Georgia sat at the nurses' station surrounded by text-books and research papers—everything she could find on what they were proposing to do to save Ms. Jenkins' life—pushing through the fatigue of the last twelve hours. She called Tom and Vicki, but the phone rang until the machine came on. She called Tom's crummy old cell and got no answer there either, so she left a message. "It's me. Call me when you get in with an update on Shawna, please."

Matt walked up to her and rubbed her neck. She knew it was him from the touch of his hand and the scent of his cologne. She tensed at his presence, not only remembering the argument they'd had earlier but because they were at work for everyone to see.

He leaned down and whispered into her ear. "I did it. I spoke with California and got permission to use Ms. Jenkins for our first human trial. I explained the risk of losing ten years of research if the media found out about our reluctance to help a patient in our own hospital. I also highlighted the impact of the cure this study offered the human race and that it far outweighed the first human trial happening in New York instead of California." She relaxed into his touch, feeling hopeful for the first time in days, and searched his face for assurance that he was serious. He smiled and his eyes lit up with the same joy she was sure was obvious on her face.

"How long to grow her cells?"

"I took the liberty of starting them off yesterday morning after you blackmailed me. We're good to go tomorrow."

She stood and gave him a hug. "Oh my God! Thank you, Matt!"

"Don't thank me yet. We still have to keep her stable until then, and there's a little issue about signing a consent form. Any idea who will do that?"

"I'll do it. I'm her attending physician, and this is an emergency procedure. She's already signed consent for her mitral valve replacement and consented to the risks of surgery." Her mind raced at the prospect of stabilizing Ms. Jenkins long term. "Let me call Joe and tell him to stay home. I'll stay here with her and make sure she survives the night. You go babysit those cells. Oh, and get someone to check in on Gus at your place. The poor dog is probably getting used to the lap of luxury over there."

Georgia dialed Joe's cell phone and caught him in time. "Well, I sure would be glad to have a decent meal tonight," he said. "You sure you can handle it, Dr. L.?"

"I'll be fine, get some rest," she said.

Georgia dialed Tom and Vicki's house again and there was still no answer. That's odd, where was Emma? Had they taken her downtown too? She dialed Tom's ancient flip phone.

"Tom Evans."

"Tom, it's Georgia. How did it go with Shawna?"

"She's a pure delight. We took her out to dinner and we're driving into the garage now."

"I was half expecting you to come by the hospital." She tried to mask the disappointment in her voice.

"We thought Shawna needed a break. She was there this morning and all. She needs some time to be a kid, away from the hospital."

"I see. Tell her we have a new plan for her mom. She's hanging in for us and things are looking up. And thanks again, Tom."

"No problem." Tom hung up.

Georgia focused on Ms. Jenkins. She ordered some fresh lab reports and some more medication. She asked for a referral from an anesthesiologist for optimal settings on the ventilator. Then she sat at the bedside and held Sandra's hand again, listening to the rhythmic breath sounds and heartbeats, tracking the second hand's march around on the clock.

Her cell phone buzzed un her lab coat pocket. It was Tom again. "Miss the sound of my voice already?" Georgia said as she answered.

"Emma's not here. All her stuff is still in her room, her cell phone, her wallet." The panic in Tom's voice made Georgia's heart race. "There's a broken window and the flower beds under it are all trashed. We've called the cops. They're on their way, but we can't keep Shawna here tonight. We have to go out and find Emma."

Chapter 19

Georgia felt the room spin and sat down in the closest chair behind the desk. She was sure they had got Emma back to a better place. Could she have spiraled off track again so soon? Georgia's hands went cold. The killer couldn't get to Georgia because she hadn't been alone. Could he have gone after the person she was closest to in the world? She was up against someone who knew her well enough to know her every move, someone close enough to her to know who she was dating and who her friends were—no, who her family was. Why the hell was she putting up with this shit? She couldn't stand for someone picking on her family. Not Emma, she's going through enough right now.

She understood that Matt didn't want the cops involved in the cells gone missing to protect his study, and she didn't really take slashed tires seriously enough at the time. But the heart on her doorstep. The notes. Then the image of Ken lying dead in his apartment flashed in her head and she imagined Emma lying in his place. No clinical trial was worth burying her best friend, the only sister she'd ever known.

"Georgia, you still there?" Tom said.

"I can't go anywhere right now, Ms. Jenkins is too unstable. I'll send Emma's boyfriend Joe over to pick Shawna up. She can stay in the on-call room with me tonight. Don't tell social services, whatever you do. Joe will help you find Emma." She was about to hang up, then added, "Tom, I'm sending over a guy named Vince to have a look at the house. He's a PI working for us—um, for me—right now on something. Answer any questions he has."

"Georgia, you're not making any sense. Why do you have a PI working for you?" Tom said.

"You don't have time for the explanation and neither do I. Go find Emma."

She hung up and dialed Joe's cell phone and gave him the directions to Tom and Vicki's house. She assured him he'd get extra brownie points toward the attending position if he was her bitch tonight and asked no questions. He gladly agreed. Then she dialed Vince and gave him Tom and Vicki's address as well.

Georgia leaned her head on the desk and took some deep breaths. Usually, she was so good in a crisis. As far as shitstorms go, this was the motherlode.

She yelled over to the nurses, "I'm running up to my office for a second. I'll be right back."

She was going to find the cards officers Richards and Hall gave her. Enough playing games. How stupid could she have been to go along with some mafia private investigator instead of the police? She needed all the help she could get.

* * *

An hour later Georgia stood in Ms. Jenkins' room looking over the most recent blood tests and double-checking the ventilator setting when she heard a tap on the window. Matt stood outside the window, a mix of fear and anger etched on his face. He motioned her to come out. Georgia left the room to meet him.

Matt whispered, "Vince called to say he's doing all he can, but the cops are tighter than the Virgin Mary about Emma's disappearance. Mind telling me what the fuck he's talking about?"

"Emma's been kidnapped." She should have texted him to let him know, but she just didn't have the time or the brain space to think of anything or anyone else.

"Why are the cops all over it?" he asked.

"Because Emma has been kidnapped, you moron. She's my best friend. Someone broke into my foster parent's house and took her. What else do you expect them to do but call the cops?"

"Vince said that the footprint outside her window looked like a disposable slip-on they wear over shoes in the operating room. It's likely our same guy."

"No shit, Sherlock." She threw her hand up in exasperation.

"Hey, I'm not the enemy here. Ken was my colleague and my friend, you know," Matt said.

"And the cops were called on that one too, right? Which is why I called the detectives working on Ken's case."

"You did what?" All the softness escaped his tone and his face in an instant.

"Emma. Has. Been. Kidnapped." Georgia clapped out the words. "If the police had been on top of this from the start, my family wouldn't be in danger."

Joe tapped Georgia on the shoulder with Shawna standing next to him. "I couldn't help but overhear. I think I know where Emma is. We had a little tiff on the phone this afternoon. Don't bother more cops with this, you don't want them asking questions about why Shawna is here, and we need the stem cell research to be accessible. I'll go to Emma."

"There they are now." Matt pointed to two officers at the nursing station asking the clerk for Georgia.

Joe left. Georgia turned back to Matt and Shawna. She told Matt to introduce Shawna to the lab animals and she'd meet him in the labs in a few minutes.

By the time the police met Georgia, she stood alone facing them, trying to make up her mind about what to say.

Chapter 20

Matt turned on the lights in the animal room and the place came to life with grunts and squeaks. There was a full bank of cages on the wall on one side of the room and farther down was the pigpen. The room was equipped with extra ventilation to keep the smell down, and the undergraduate students had the luxurious job of cleaning out the bedding every day. He may feel like Old MacDonald every once in a while, but this certainly didn't look or smell like any farm he'd been on as a kid.

"This is the fun part of my job. I get to play with animals."

"Wow. You have lots of them in here," Shawna said.

"Not as many as we'd like, but we don't want them overcrowded either because this is the only space we have for them. Luckily, the mice don't take up too much room, and we have lots of them."

They walked over to a wall full of mouse cages and another with ribbit cages.

"Do you want to feed the rabbits? These ones over here are on a high-calorie diet to test some diabetic medications, so the more you feed them the better for our study." He handed her some lettuce and apple slices.

"Thanks." The poor girl looked exhausted. So much going on for such a young person.

"I bet your life has been pretty crazy lately, hey?" He couldn't imagine the stress this girl had been under with her mom hanging on by a thread. He remembered how difficult it was for him as an adult while his fiancée fought for every breath.

"Mom's been sick for almost a year now, but since she came to the hospital this last time, it's been nuts."

"You know Dr. Laurence has been trying very hard to find a way to make your mom better. She's taken a real liking to both of you. I can see why." He smiled at the back of her braided head.

"What is it you do? I mean, what do you do with people? Or do you just test animals?" Shawna asked.

"My most important study involves Mildred over here."

"A pig?"

"Pigs' hearts are very similar to human hearts," Matt explained. "I'm actually working on a study that uses stem cells to regenerate heart tissue. Exactly what your mother needs."

"Really? Then why are we waiting for a heart transplant? Why not use your stem cells?"

Matt met Shawna's big brown eyes and melted at the directness of her question. Why were they waiting, indeed?

"We plan to implant the stem cells tomorrow. I'm waiting for them to finish reproducing in my laboratory."

"Can I see them?"

"You'd rather visit with cells in a petri dish than farm animals?"

She laughed. "I'm thirteen, not three. Show me how you help sick people instead."

"The room is right down the hall," Matt said.

He turned off the lights and led the way to the other room. He keyed in the code for the door and unlocked the extra padlock Vince had added. Maintenance was not happy about the lack of access to the lab for cleaning, but Matt had assured them it was temporary. He needed those cells to be safe.

Matt opened the fridge, grabbed the petri dish, and slid it under a microscope. "Wow."

"What?" Shawna took over the eyepiece. "What's wow? What am I looking at?"

"You're looking at enough cells to implant tonight, my dear. We're going to save your mother's life right now."

* * *

Georgia shook Officer Richards' and Officer Hall's hands and led the way for them to exit the surgical ICU, impressed with her ability to invent a completely fictitious story on the spot. "Again, I do apologize for wasting any of your time, I didn't realize that Ken's death had nothing to do with the fact that I secretly slept with him at the Christmas party last year. I won't bother you anymore."

"Call us if you think of anything pertinent," Hall said, his words dripping with passive aggression.

"Good evening," Richards said.

She rubbed the back of her neck as she made her way to Ms. Jenkins' bedside. The monitor started ringing again. She silenced the monitor and held Sandra's hand.

"Hey there, I've got a visitor for you. Shawna's here. I'll get her to come and say hi." She yelled over her shoulder, "Can somebody find Dr. Mancini and Shawna, please?"

"They're coming down the hall now." A faceless voice yelled back.

"There you go, Shawna's here to see you, everything is going to be okay. Hang in there."

Matt wheeled in a metal trolley filled with instruments and trays, clanging his way through the room.

"Shawna, come talk to your mom. She's having a hard time and maybe your voice with help give her some strength," Georgia said.

"Can I speak with you out here for a minute, Dr. Laurence?" Matt asked.

They walked out of the room, leaving Shawna to comfort her mom while the respiratory therapist fiddled with the ventilator settings again.

"Matt, she's not going to make it until morning. I'm losing her." Georgia wanted to cry in his arms but kept her professional composure for Shawna's sake.

"I've got the cells. We're implanting them now." He smiled at her.

"How? Why? You said they weren't ready."

"Shawna wanted to see them and I realized that we have more than enough. We need to do this. I need to stop dragging my ass when there's a life at stake. Now, get me an ultrasound machine and gown up, we're saving a life tonight." Matt squared her shoulders.

"Oh, Matt!" She hugged him then shouted the order to the closest nurse to page radiology for an ultrasound machine stat.

At the bedside, the whole nursing staff was primed and ready to go. Georgia held Shawna's shoulders and explained the procedure to her, then led her to the nurses' lunchroom where the TV on the wall played Doctor Who.

Georgia said she'd find something more appropriate, but Shawna stopped her. "No, I need to get caught up. This is my mom's favorite show. I want to be able to tell her what happened when she wakes up."

"Okay. I'll send somebody for you when the procedure's done."

Georgia walked into the room where the respiratory tech stood beside his ventilator. Donna, ready to assist, held open a sterile gown for Georgia.

"Donna, can I have a syringe with some Versed ready?"

"Already on the tray for you Dr. L."

"Thanks," Georgia said.

"This isn't going to be very long, Georgia, you may be

better off with a bolus of propofol, since she's on the ventilator anyway," Matt said.

"Okay. Milk of amnesia it is." Donna said as she keyed in the bolus on the propofol's continuous drip.

Georgia noticed Matt was awfully sexy in scrubs, gowned and masked. His smoldering eyes gazed into hers and he gave a quick wink. "Ready to go," he said.

"Inject away," Georgia said.

Matt spread out a sterile field over Ms. Jenkins' chest wound and squirted blue conductive gel to the left of the incision. He applied the ultrasound wand while everyone stared at the screen attached to the machine.

"Whoa, you weren't kidding about the condition of her heart muscle, were you?" Matt said.

"I don't bullshit people, you should know that about me by now," Georgia replied.

"Okay, I'll go through the incision and diagonally pass the sternum to the left ventricle. Right there. You see it?"

"Sounds good to me," Georgia said.

"Can you hold the ultrasound wand while I do the injection?"

Georgia walked around to the same side of the bed as Matt. She couldn't believe how warm and tingly she felt working next to him. Of all the inappropriate times to be distracted by feelings.

She took the wand from Matt and kept darting her eyes between all the monitors, watching the slow rise and fall of the multicolored waves of her heartbeat, breathing and oxygen levels.

Matt pushed the long metal needle past the sternum and angled it to the heart. It appeared on the ultrasound and Matt used the image to guide him to the right spot in the ventricle, where he injected the cells without completely puncturing through the wall or hitting the heart arteries. All that practice on pigs had paid off.

"Looking good," Matt said.

When he slowly withdrew the syringe, the heart started fibrillating on the ultrasound monitor and immediately alarmed the heart monitor.

"Shit, that's V-fib," Georgia said. "Get me the crash cart, Donna. Apparently, her heart doesn't like to be poked at. Turn off the balloon pump and get her off the ventilator, I'm zapping her."

"I think it was the irritation," Matt said.

"Whatever. Charge to two hundred." Georgia applied the paddles to each side of Sandra's chest. All eyes turned to the monitor. "Clear." No change.

"Ah, fuck it all. Three-sixty. Clear," Georgia said.

"We've got sinus brady and a weak pulse," Donna called out.

"One milligram of atropine, push," Georgia ordered, preparing to do chest compression if necessary.

"Here we go," said Matt. "The heart rate is coming up and so is her blood pressure."

"Get her on the ventilator and get me a set of blood gases in half an hour, electrolytes, and a CBC while you're at it," Georgia said. She turned to Matt. "Your pigs all code when you gave the injections?"

"Only the last one."

"Maybe you should have mentioned that to me, you idiot."

"I thought it was a fluke," he said. "Obviously, I'm at the start of the human trials and I might have to perfect my technique a bit more."

"I would say so. When do we expect your miracle to work?" Georgia realized that she probably should have asked that before. What if Ms. Jenkins couldn't hang on until the cells started reproducing and strengthening her heart?

"I don't know what to expect in a human heart. Usually two days with the pigs before some cardiac output improvement. A week-and-a-half for a full recovery."

Georgia stared at the tray where the empty syringe lay on its side. She'd just learned about the possibility of those cells, yet it felt like she'd been waiting to use them for so long it hardly seemed real. She grabbed the other syringe full of Versed and stuck it in her lab coat pocket just in case Ms. Jenkins coded again. The minute it would take to draw up the medication could save her life.

Matt took off his gloves. "Now for the fun part—paperwork and waiting."

Chapter 21

Georgia stared at her cell phone every two minutes, waiting for a phone call from Tom or Vince or anybody. She set up Shawna and herself in the resident's on-call room with the ancient portable teaching TV and DVD player and the nurses' stash of old movies. Shawna chose Casablanca. One of the nurses even got some chips and sodas from the vending machines for them. They sat side by side on their twin beds munching away, a pair of teens on a sleepover.

Matt had gone home to put the dog out for a bit. He said he'd be back after a shower and change of clothes, but Georgia insisted she could handle the night shift and to meet her in the morning with a latte and a croissant instead.

After pretending to watch the movie for half an hour, Georgia said she was going to check on how Brian was taking care of her number one patient, but she really needed to talk to somebody about Emma.

First, she called Tom's cell. "Hey, what's the latest?"

"Nothing new to report. Your PI left a while ago, asked for the keys to Emma's place. Vicki wasn't very keen on handing them over, but she finally did. He also looked in her cell phone history and purse. Much more thoroughly than the cops, I might add. They're treating this like a runaway because of her past drug use. They think it's a relapse."

"Where are you now?" she asked.

"On my way home from talking to all her old dealer friends and visiting her old hangouts. Nobody's seen her in a few years."

"That's good in a way, I guess," Georgia said.

"I'm calling it a night and praying she comes home. I'll keep you posted."

"Thanks." She hung up and dialed Vince. "It's Dr. Laurence. What's new on Emma's kidnapping?"

"I've got three of my guys out searching for her. I got no prints off your heart gift box, but they've confirmed it was a human heart. And I checked out Emma's apartment. Her phones aren't bugged and there's no sign of someone sneaking in. I checked the place with UV light. It's been cleaned recently but I found some body fluids on the headboard, walls, and carpets. She was a very busy lady recently, but no visible blood anywhere or sign of any struggle," Vince said.

"She has a new boyfriend. I doubt anyone would be following her home with him there all the time." Georgia tried to sift through everything Vince had just dumped on her.

"Our perp has been following her and you and Dr. Mancini. They've probably been following her boyfriend too. It has to be somebody you work with or somebody Matt works with," his raspy voice concluded.

"Are my parents safe?" Georgia couldn't live with herself if something happened to them too.

"I have a guy parked outside their house tonight, and a guy watching you in the hospital."

"How? I don't see any Mafioso bodyguard types around here."

"I'm not an amateur, gorgeous. Gino will look like all the other night staff maintenance men."

"Thanks for all of this," Georgia said.

"No worries, Dr. Mancini's family are important clients, and they pay very well. I will have a full report for you and Dr. Mancini in his office tomorrow morning around nine. I'll call if anything comes up before then."

Vince suggesting that Joe could also be followed made Georgia realize for the first time that Joe might also be in danger. He was her right-hand man the same as Ken had been Matt's go-to guy, and he was Emma's boyfriend. She had to give him the full story and have him watch his back. Maybe he could come to the hospital where they had the protection of Gino the inconspicuous maintenance man.

She dialed Joe's cell phone. "Hey, Joe. Any luck?"

"No. Nothing."

"We'll find her, and then you can kiss and make up," Georgia said, wanting to reassure him.

"Okay, sure," Joe said. She was concerned he didn't have a smartass comment for her.

"Listen, Matt hired a PI and we think you might be in some danger. There's a goon here protecting us tonight. You should come and stay at the hospital."

"I'll be fine," his clipped tone sounded almost robotic. "How's Jenkins?"

"Oh, she's great. Matt gave her the stem cells and besides coding during the procedure, she's stabilized and she's holding her own."

"He what?" Joe yelled.

"She's okay, apparently it happened with his pig too. He finally got California to okay her as the first human trial. Isn't he the best?"

"Yeah, the best. See you."

The line went dead, and Georgia had a sense of unease wash over her. There was something in his voice. Was he pissed about missing the procedure? Was he pissed about Emma? She couldn't shake the feeling there was more to his distant tone and the sudden end to their call.

Chapter 22

Emma drifted awake again and sat, curled up in the dark and cold room. Her head pounded to the rhythm of her heart. She pressed her back against a tiled wall. She didn't know where she was, all she knew was that she was alone. The smell in the air held a hint of death with an undertone of industrial sterilizer.

She felt around the floor beside her and found a small metal wheel. Her hand continued up the leg to a gurney. She ran her hand along the top of the gurney and felt a blanket covering a plastic bag containing a cold hard mass.

She recoiled her hand and sat down again as her dizzy, foggy brain pieced together where she was: a morgue. The sudden influx of bile in her mouth rivaled the metallic taste from whatever drug she'd been given to knock her out.

Drugs. More drugs.

If she made it out of this place alive, she swore she'd ensure her body was the purest temple. No man was worth the vileness pulsing through her body. Though she wasn't entirely convinced that staying on her mental health regimen over the last month could have helped much with being drugged into submission and kidnapped.

She tried to piece together what happened and all she could recall was being alone in the house. She was lying in bed reading a novel—a flash of blue from a latex-gloved hand—her face covered with a towel—sharp shooting pain in her arm. Then, everything faded to black. She lifted her hand to her arm now and all that was left was a sore bruise.

Latex gloves, an arm injection, and sitting in a morgue.

She sure as hell hoped this meant that someone from the hospital was responsible for kidnapping her and that Joe or Georgia would be able to find her and the kidnapper soon.

She found it odd that she'd be taken and dumped. She wasn't bound or gagged. She could just stand up and walk out, couldn't she?

Those must have been powerful drugs if it took her what felt like a good half an hour after waking up to figure out that she actually could leave. She had no idea how long she'd been there, but it was time to get out.

She stood gingerly, feeling her way around the walls in order to avoid the sea of gurneys, which she tried to imagine didn't hold dead bodies. One wall contained a metal counter and cupboards with sliding glass doors. The next contained handles on rows and columns of refrigerator doors. On the next wall, she found a light switch. Once the room was illuminated and the splitting pain in her head subsided enough to allow her to open her eyes, her location was confirmed. The morgue spillover room. She immediately tried the door but it was locked from the outside.

She took in the sea of dead bodies around her. Many of them had their body bags opened and their chests cut open. One had only a cavernous hole where a heart should have been. She turned to the door again and started to pound and scream.

* * *

Georgia dosed fitfully waking with a start but the only sound in the room was the rhythmic release of Shawna's breaths. Her mind ran through every move she'd made over the last week, every interaction she'd had with every person she knew, and came up empty. She couldn't stay asleep when Emma could be lying cold and starving somewhere if she wasn't already dead.

Her cell vibrated. It was a text from Matt.

4:03 a.m.: On my way to the hospital.

She got up and ran her fingers through her hair, threw a piece of gum in her mouth, and headed out of the room to call him.

"You're up way early this morning."

"I couldn't sleep. How's Ms. Jenkins doing?" Matt asked.

"The same. Stable, but her numbers aren't changing drastically yet."

"We don't want drastic. Tomorrow, we'll see a bit of a difference."

"Did you get my latte?"

"Crap, I knew there was something else for me to do. I'm so distracted by all this craziness with Ken dead and Emma's disappearance. I tell you, I was sure I was being followed to work this morning," Matt said, whispering by the end.

"It could have been one of Vince's guys," Georgia said. "He said he's got somebody on my parents' house and someone here too. Let me grab a couple of coffees from the vending machine and meet you in your office. We can brainstorm together instead of both of us thinking around in circles."

"Sure. To be honest, I hated spending the night apart," his voice faltered, "I want you close. It would make me feel a lot better to have you next to me. To know you're safe."

* * *

Matt couldn't believe he just confessed to Georgia how much he longed to be with her. Not that it wasn't true, but he had no idea where they stood in their relationship—or if they even had one. Gus seemed to think so. Her dog treated him with as much reverence as he felt for Georgia.

He keyed in the code to the lab and checked on his locked fridge. Everything seemed to be in the right order.

Reassured about his lab, his thoughts went right back to Georgia. Did he really want to spend every waking minute by her side? That was why he came back to the hospital at four in the morning, wasn't it? That was also why he threw all his weight into helping Ms. Jenkins. To help a patient, sure, but more to impress that patient's surgeon. After one week of having Georgia call him every four-letter word in the book, of having her on his ass about handing over the cells even when the study could be compromised—a week in which a close friend was murdered—all he could think about was securing a future with Georgia Laurence. A long, loving, passionate future by her side. There was no denying it, he was falling in love with her.

Matt walked over to the animal holding room to check in on Mildred. He flicked on a few lamps so as not to disturb the nocturnal scurry of the mice. He bent over to give the pig a scratch and stood up to find Joe Carter standing beside him in the near dark.

"Whoa, man. You shouldn't sneak up on people like that." Matt smiled and patted Joe on the shoulder. "You been by the SICU to visit our latest victory against heart disease?"

"No, I came straight here to shake the hand of the miracle maker," Joe said.

"Aw, come on. It's no miracle. It's been seven long years of tedious science."

"No, no. You don't get to stand there and be humble about taking away my chance to stand out and impress my boss," Joe said, stepping out of the shadows.

"What are you talking about?" For the first time, Matt noticed Joe's creased forehead and wild eyes. The guy turned Matt's blood to ice.

"There's one attending position here in Our Lady of Grace. Only one fucking job," said Joe. He practically spat the words. "I needed that job if I was going to have Emma. I needed to implant those cells and save Dr. Laurence's favorite patient. But no, you had to do it first. You were already fucking the whore, so why did you have to steal my recognition, my job, and my chance at a happy life with my girl?"

Matt grabbed Joe by the shirt and gave a low growl. "Watch your mouth, asshole." He shoved Joe back toward the middle of the room. Light bounced off metal. Joe held a scalpel in his hand. Matt backed up a few paces but was cornered between the pen gate and the wall.

"You see, Dr. Mancini, this whole fiasco was an error on my part. I should have eliminated any possible interference from the start. From the time I met Ken and he showed me your research, I thought your expertise would have been of use to me, but I was clearly wrong. I should have killed you instead of Ken. Before he was on to me and started asking questions. But that's all past now, isn't it? I have what I want now. I have Emma, and we're going to take off together and make a new life far away from her meddling family with their fucking made-up diagnosis and treatment and that controlling bitch of a foster sister." Joe thrust the scalpel near Matt's face making him flinch. "Yeah, that's right, your girlfriend's a whore and a controlling bitch, and she'll never see her sister again as long as I'm alive to prevent it. And you, doctor, will not be alive to help Georgia find Emma either."

In an instant, Matt knew without a doubt that he loved Georgia and would do anything to save her—and her sister. The last few days flashed before his eyes and he realized how insignificant personal recognition for his scientific work was compared to the cure his study offered to Ms. Jenkins and Shawna and the human race. Joe's scalpel had forced a focus on his priorities: to cure heart disease and spend his life with Georgia. Everything else blurred into a pixelated background.

A noise from the hall startled them both. Matt's already racing heart accelerated. Georgia was on her way with coffee.

Chapter 23

"What the fuck is going on here?" Georgia had expected to find Matt scratching a pig belly, not being held at knifepoint by her chief resident.

As soon as Joe heard her curse, he pulled Matt to his chest and put the scalpel to his taller and more muscular victim's carotid artery. Her pulse raced into a roar in her ears but not solely from fear. A very large part of her was furious.

"There goes your residency, shit-for-brains," she said, fighting to keep her voice steady. "Get the scalpel away from the poor guy's neck and get out of my hospital."

"Georgia, he's got Emma," Matt spat out before Joe pulled him closer and drew a droplet of blood on the scalpel's blade.

That changed everything. She didn't mind shooting off her mouth if it meant provoking a fight she knew Matt would easily win, but if Joe had lost his mind enough to have kidnapped Emma there was no telling where her smartass remarks could lead.

"I've got Emma and I'm keeping her," Joe said, not loosening his grip on Matt. "You and your foster family have done enough, brainwashing her into believing your bullshit. She needs to be away from you controlling people, not in a fucking yoga class. You should know better, Dr. Laurence, you're a surgeon. I have bent over backward to impress you into giving me the attending position so I can be with Emma. Well, fuck you and your stem cell gigolo. I'm making my own destiny. And it starts with getting rid of pig-man right here and now."

"Wait." Georgia put up her hands like she was being held at gunpoint.

"Wait? For what? You think I'm going to stand here and give you time for a loving goodbye? You're lucky I'm leaving you behind as punishment, so you can mourn your boyfriend here and miss your sister for the rest of your life, but I'm not going to give you the privilege of a sappy farewell." Joe spat while he spoke.

"He's not my boyfriend, Joe. You can still have the position," she said, choosing her words slowly, carefully. "You were always the one I was going to recommend. I told you that in the OR. I love Emma too much to send you away. I love Emma more than I could ever love some second-rate laboratory-dwelling excuse for a doctor. But I can't hire you if I watch you kill him in front of me. I'd be a material witness. Take me to Emma right now and you can do what you want with Matt once she's safe in my arms. Just bring me to Emma, please. She must be terrified." Georgia inched closer and avoided Matt's eyes.

"How do I know I can trust you?" Joe asked.

"You can trust that Emma will never be happy if she can't see me and our parents ever again. I'm telling you that Matt and his study mean nothing to me. We got what we needed from him. You know how much more important Emma is to all of us."

Joe looked down at Mildred, lost in thought for a second while he weighed his options. "I'll bring you down to Emma, but you call the CEO with your decision to hire me right then and there. I'll dispose of Matt once the call is made."

"Deal," Georgia said.

"Do I get a say in any of this?" Matt slipped in, his voice barely above a whisper.

"No," they both replied. Matt swallowed, his face pale as

a sheet. Shit, he'd believed every word she said. How could he think she didn't care about his life?

"Move," Joe ordered as he shoved Matt forward into the hall, scalpel digging into his back through his shirt. He pushed them to the freight elevator at the back of the wing. Georgia followed closely behind, mentally running through the procedure for repairing a severed carotid artery. She shoved her hand into her lab coat pocket to hide its violent shaking. Her fingers found the syringe of Versed. The perfect drug to knock out a patient for an unpleasant procedure—or a crazed doctor holding a man hostage with a scalpel. The cold metal elevator doors opened into the morgue.

"She is still alive, right?" Georgia said.

Joe chuckled.

How could she have missed all the signs of working with a complete sociopath all these years? Had he always been psychotic or was his obsession with Emma what pushed him over the edge?

Georgia needed the perfect opportunity to stick Joe with the sedative. She had to have Emma near and Matt away from the scalpel. Keeping her hand in her pocket, she uncapped the needle and held the barrel in her palm with her thumb at the plunger.

* * *

Matt battled in his mind between fear, rage, and disappointment. How could what he had with Georgia mean so little to her that she'd sacrifice him for her sister's well-being? Now that she had the cure in her patient's chest, he was useless to her. Worst, she referred to him as a second-rate doctor stuck in a lab, exactly what his father had always called him.

He couldn't even hold Georgia's gaze. She'd broken his heart. She played right into Joe's game to let her patient and her sister live another day, at the expense of his own life and sacrificing the possibilities his cure offered heart disease sufferers the world over. That wasn't the Georgia he knew. Nothing made sense.

Joe shoved him against the wall near a door and stuck the scalpel to his chest.

"Right there between the fifth and sixth rib is your heart. I'll carve it right out of your chest if you so much as flinch while I get Emma. You hear me?"

It took everything in Matt's power not to spit in the man's face.

Joe transferred the scalpel to his left hand and heaved his elbow into Matt's gut, knocking the wind out of him at the same time as Joe reached into his scrubs' side pocket for the key to the door. He barely had a chance to catch his breath from the blow before Georgia was shouting in his face. "Get down!"

The blur that followed included her driving a needle into Joe's arm, a sharp pain slicing across Matt's abdomen, Georgia shoving Joe, then the crack of Joe's head hitting the tiled wall.

Joe was on all fours calling Georgia some choice names when she kicked him in the ribs and flattened him.

"Where did he drop the key?" Georgia knelt on Joe to keep him immobilized while she felt around for the master key. Matt was about to answer but thought maybe he should have a seat for a second. The room started to spin. He slid down the wall.

"Oh shit, you're bleeding." Georgia ripped open Matt's shirt to find a deep gash across his abdomen. She took off her lab coat and balled it into a compress.

"Do you have your cell on you?" she asked.

"No, it's on my desk. There's a phone. Down the hall."

"I'm not leaving you here bleeding to death with the chance that shit face might wake up."

"You didn't seem to care if I lived or died a few minutes ago." He fought the darkness creeping into his peripheral vision.

"You stupid jerk. That was an act so I could get to Emma." Relief washed over him while his extremities went numb.

"Then get Emma. I'll wait here if that's okay with you."

* * *

Georgia found the key and opened the door. Emma was curled up right inside, sitting balled up, rocking on her heels.

"Emma, it's Georgia. You're okay now. Let's get out of here." Georgia immediately regretted every harsh word she threw at Emma this week. She was the best friend and sister she could have ever asked for. The last thing she deserved was to be locked up by the man she loved.

"Oh, Georgia—" She started to cry in spasmodic breaths of relief. "Are we safe? What's going on? Who did this?"

"Don't you worry about Joe. I've got him taken care of for a while. Come on. We need to get to a phone," Georgia said.

"Joe? Why would I worry about Joe?"

She pulled Emma out of the morgue's overflow room and pushed her to face away from the two men lying to the right. She glanced over her shoulder to find her makeshift compression pad saturated with blood. She held Emma's wrist and pulled her into a sprint to the phone down the hall.

"Operator, I need a code blue called for the morgue anteroom, security, and an overhead for Gino from maintenance. Yes, specifically Gino." She sat Emma in the office swivel chair at the desk.

"When the code team comes, send them to the morgue spillover room."

"Don't leave me alone, Georgie, please," Emma begged.

"I'm only down the hall here. This place will be full of people in a few minutes. I need to help Matt."

Georgia ran to Matt, who was still slumped on the floor. He lifted a heavy eyelid when she called his name but seemed to have difficulty focusing on her. She darted into the holding room and grabbed a sheet off a corpse.

"I'm so sorry, Matt. I thought you were clear of the scalpel. I didn't want you to get hurt. I'm sorry I used you as bait." Georgia removed the now-red lab coat compress and replaced it with the folded sheet, applying as much pressure as she could to the wound.

"It's okay. Promise me the research gets published," Matt murmured.

"Don't you lie there and tell me to promise you shit about the future," she said. "I'm not going to let you die from a little flesh wound, mister. I'm a heart surgeon. I save lives. I love you too much to let a simple little cut kill you."

"You love me?"

"Of course, I love you, you nimrod!"

"I love you too."

She never thought she'd utter those words, or hear them for that matter. But she meant it. Matt closed his eyes and they stayed closed. Her heart sank.

The code team came running empty-handed and got a blast of hell from Georgia. "Why on Earth would there be a crash cart in the morgue? Get me a stretcher and some lap pads and gauze and call general surgery and the OR. We need to close an abdominal wound stat."

Chapter 24

Security burst into the room, followed by Gino. Security cuffed Joe and lifted him into a wheelchair. The Hippocratic Oath forced Georgia to tell them to be sure Joe didn't obstruct his own airway with his limp tongue. When they left, she updated Gino and asked him to take Emma to Vince and for them to take her home to Tom and Vicki. It pained her that Emma would be terrified of Gino and Vince, but she wasn't leaving Matt's side.

A stretcher raced toward them and three orderlies lifted Matt onto it. Georgia hopped onto the stretcher and straddled Matt, applying pressure to the abdominal wound as they wheeled to the elevator, through the hospital, to the operating room. They were met by half the surgical service who'd recently arrived to start their day. Georgia hopped off and let the team take over Matt's care. She washed Matt's blood off her hands, put on a fresh pair of scrubs, and began a pacing marathon, stopping only to annoy the circulating nurses for updates every five minutes.

After three hours of pacing and wringing her hands, she was joined by her lawyer Stuart and her boss, Dr. Douglas.

"The police have a full confession from Dr. Carter," Dr. Douglas said. "He stole the stem cells and the procedure manuals. He injected Mrs. Reynolds' heart with stem cells, causing her to bleed to death after surgery."

Georgia interjected, "The son of bitch."

Douglas continued unphased, "He confessed to killing Ken Liu. He's also displaying many symptoms of psychosis and, oddly, also withdrawal. After further questioning by the police, we've been able to piece together that he was abusing a drug he received from a clinical trial he signed up for trying to earn extra money."

"Mr. Reynolds has dropped his case against you," Stuart said. "And Marion Hammon decided to take the retirement package the hospital offered. It looks like your license to practice is safe. You're in the clear."

Georgia sat in the closest chair along the wall. She turned up to Dr. Douglas. "I'd like to take a few weeks off as soon as I know Ms. Jenkins is stable," she said. "My surgeries got pushed back this week and the urgent ones can be handled by Dr. Williams. I need to find my center again."

"That sounds like the best idea I've heard you come up with in a long time, Georgia," Dr. Douglas said. "You're a huge asset to this hospital, despite your rebellious mouth. I want you to come back rested." He gave Georgia a caring nod and both men patted her back and walked away.

The sliding doors opened to the recovery room and Matt was wheeled out of the OR on a stretcher with a bag of blood hanging and fluids running into his IV. Dr. Steve Kennedy, the trauma surgeon, followed right behind Matt to update Georgia on his condition.

"It was a severed mesenteric with lots of blood loss," Dr. Kennedy said. "But he's a healthy, athletic guy, so he should be fine. He'll need antibiotics and I suggest you treat him to a huge steak dinner next weekend to bring up his blood count."

"Thanks, Steve. I intend to feed him a huge steak every Saturday for the rest of his life." The truth of the words that just escaped her mouth washed over her. She'd never thought beyond saving Ms. Jenkins and securing Shawna's future. She'd never considered her own future—with Matt.

"That's a marriage vow any man could appreciate," Dr. Kennedy said.

Georgia walked away to keep up with Matt's stretcher, missing the opportunity to clarify the marriage vow misunderstanding. But as she walked alongside the stretcher and witnessed Matt mouth her name, and his eyes begin to flutter open, she realized she would be more than happy for that to be in their wedding vows someday.

* * *

"This is Crystal Johnston for Channel Five News, here at the cardiac surgical intensive care unit at Our Lady of Grace Hospital, with the first person to ever receive heart stem cells grown from her own skin cells. Ms. Jenkins, how are you feeling?"

"Like a brand-new person," Sandra Jenkins said under the bright lights of the TV camera.

Georgia lounged on her couch with Matt's head in her lap and Gus propped up against her side. She ran her hand through Matt's hair as they listened to the newscast. Matt had recovered well over the last two weeks, almost as quickly as Ms. Jenkins herself. She'd followed up on Ms. Jenkins in her time off and was utterly astonished by how well she recuperated. Georgia had a sneaking suspicion that Matt's recovery dragged because he preferred sleeping in her bed and having her tend to his wounds in her own special way.

They'd just hung up from their daily call with Emma and Shawna, who were bonding nicely, having taken over Tom and Vicki's home and turned it into a perpetual mixture of intellectual conversation and giggle sessions. Emma was going to be seeing a therapist for a little longer to recover from the kidnapping trauma, but having Shawna around was healing to her as well.

Matt turned onto his back and gave her one of his dead sexy smiles.

"What?" Georgia had kept her libido in check while Matt healed, and those teasing stares didn't help one bit.

"Nothing. Wondering if you're appreciating your role in Ms. Jenkins feeling better and Shawna's happiness."

"Listen to the news, will you?" Georgia said.

The reporter on the screen continued. "I'm told that your chances at a heart transplant were very slim due to a rare blood match that can only be found in people with ancestors from a small region of Africa. And that this is part of a clinical trial involving a research team here in New York State and their partners in Encino, California."

"That's right. My surgeon, Dr. Georgia Laurence, found a wonderful researcher, Dr. Matt Mancini, who could implant cells in my heart and have it repair itself."

"It seems Ms. Jenkins is only the first of many people suffering from heart disease who will be grateful to Dr. Matt Mancini and his stem cell research," the reporter said.

Georgia gazed into Matt's eyes and smiled.

"What?" he said.

"Wondering if you're appreciating your role in curing the world of heart disease."

"Kiss me, will you?"

Acknowledgments

The biggest thank you has to go to my family—Rod, Sarah, Victoria, Mitchell, and Anderson—who gave me the time and space to write knowing it was part of what makes me whole and a better mom and wife. I am indebted to all my romance writing colleagues from Ottawa that educated and inspired me from the beginning of my taking writing seriously. Thank you for your first critiques Brenda Heald and Linda Poitevin.

This book is what it is because of the loyal friendship and distribution expertise from LeeAnn Lessard of Lachesis Publishing. You have always been just a phone call away to answer my questions and encourage my dreams. I am forever grateful to my red pen maven and editor extraordinaire, Zoey Duncan. You brought this story into the 21st century and had my feminist back every step of the way. I am beyond grateful that I get to work with Tami on more than just my book cover. I am so thankful for the beautiful job you did with my vision.

Finally, I want to acknowledge the complexities of medicine and the amazing human body. This book is being released because of the COVID-19 pandemic, specifically because I realized how much we all need a bit of a distraction and escape from real life and its constant breaking news stories. Who would have guessed that, with all the supporters I have in my life, it would take a virus to push me to publish? I wish I could remember the name of the journalist who did a story on stem cell research in cardiac care who gave me the idea for this story ten years ago, but to him and all the healthcare professionals working to advance medical care, thank you.

About the Author

Tammy Plunkett left her career as a registered nurse to stay home and raise her four children. It turned out that she could only take so much Sesame Street and returned to her first love—writing. Tammy spent a few years working solely in fiction then switched gears to non-fiction while she practiced as a life coach and writing coach. After her third child came out as transgender, she focused her work on helping parents of transgender kids, blogging, and writing mainstream articles. She continues to return to her love of writing in both fiction and non-fiction. When not at her keyboard, Tammy can be found hiking with her family in the Canadian Rocky Mountains.

CPSIA information can be obtained
at www.ICGtesting.com
Printed in the USA
LVHW012132290920
667424LV00002B/276